PUBLISHER'S NOTE

This is the fifth volume of Charlie Small's journal and was discovered by a team of archaeologists who were excavating a site before the builders moved in to put up a new block of flats. It was lucky they did, or this incredible document would now be lost under tons of concrete!

Intrigued by their find, Dr Septimus Vole, the chief archaeologist, examined the journal carefully. He came to the same conclusion as the publishers: Charlie Small's journals seem to be completely genuine.

Hearing of this new discovery, the publishers asked if they could add it to their growing collection of chronicles describing Charlie Small's incredible adventures. Dr Vole readily agreed and all the volumes are now in the possession of Mr Nick Ward, custodian of the Charlie Small journals.

Alongside this book, the archaeologists found some other items: an enormous crocodile's tooth and a broken telescope. We know from reading Charlie's previous adventures that they are part of his trusty explorer's kit. He must have lost them and, knowing how careful he is with all his adventurer's tools, we can only hope that he has not had some terrible accident – or been captured by some horrible foe ...

Because of this, the publishers have decided to mount an expedition to search for Charlie Small. We will not be happy until we learn of his whereabouts and, if possible, bring him back home. What follows is a note from the leader of the expedition.

The Charlie Small Relief Expedition

Where is Charlie Small? Can we find him and help him get home? How can you be eight years old and four hundred years old at the same time? Are Charlie's journals telling the truth, or is this the most elaborate hoax of the century?

These are just some of the questions everyone has been asking, and the publishers of Charlie Small's amazing journals are determined to find the answers! As custodian of the journals and finder of the very first Charlie Small diary, I have been asked to head an expedition and go in search of the lost boy adventurer.

After spending months poring over maps, I am finally ready. I have hired a team of porters to carry my explorer's equipment on the expedition. I have packed tents and stoves;

food and satellite navigation systems; guns and ammo; bows and arrows.

We don't know which river Charlie set out on, but I've decided to start my journey where I found his first journal. I'll sail all the way to the coast and then, if I still haven't found him, take a ship across the wide tumbling oceans. Will I find a clue to the whereabouts of our hero, Charlie Small? I hope so!

I will send regular e-mails to let you know how I'm getting on, so please check the website **www.charliesmall.co.uk** for any updates. Our boats are loaded and we're ready to start. Ouch! I've just got a splinter from the side of our boat. This adventuring lark might be more dangerous than I thought. Wish me luck!

Mr Nickelodious Trumpery Ward

(Nick Ward)

GENTLEMAN EXPLORER AND
CUSTODIAN OF THE CHARLIE SMALL JOURNALS

oh no - it's
all gone dark!

Man-cha!

THE
AMAZING ADVENTURES OF
CHARLIE SMALL (400)

Notebook 5

Da dum,
da dum!

CHARLIE
IN THE
UNDERWORLD

Watch out
here come
the frogs

A DAVID FICKLING BOOK

All rights reserved. Published in the United States by David Fickling Books,
an imprint of Random House Children's Books,
a division of Random House, Inc., New York.
Originally published in Great Britain by David Fickling Books,
an imprint of Random House Children's Books,
a division of the Random House Group Ltd., in 2008.

David Fickling Books and the colophon are trademarks of David Fickling.

Visit us on the Web!
www.randomhouse.com/kids

Educators and librarians, for a variety of teaching tools, visit us at
www.randomhouse.com/teachers

Library of Congress Cataloging-in-Publication Data is available upon request.
ISBN: 978-0-385-75178-0 (trade)

Printed in the United States of America

October 2009

10 9 8 7 6 5 4 3 2 1

First American Edition

NAME: Charlie Small

ADDRESS: Tom's house, Nichol Court, Castle Shadows, The Underworld

AGE: 400 (at least!)

MOBILE: 07713 1223

SCHOOL: It's so long ago I can hardly remember, but I think it was St Beckham's

THINGS I LIKE: Gorillas; practising cutlass-fighting; Braemar, Jenny and Granny Green; Wild Bob Ffrance; Nagachak and, although she is a big pest, Freecloud!

THINGS I HATE: Captain Cut-throat (a bully); the Puppet Master (a big bully); Horatio Ham (a bully and a big twit); Joseph Craik (the biggest nastiest bully of the lot); the Barbarous Bats; Mapwai

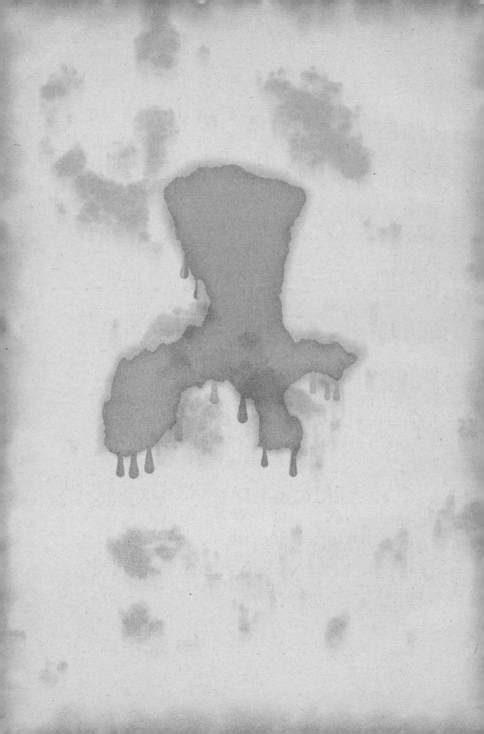

If you find this book, PLEASE look after it. This is the only true account of my remarkable adventures.

My name is Charlie Small and I am four hundred years old, maybe even more. But in all those long years I have never grown up. Something happened when I was eight years old, something I can't begin to understand. I went on a journey... and I'm still trying to find my way home. Now, although I have fought a revolting Spidion, been attacked by a monster Megashark and been trapped in tunnels a mile below the earth's surface, I still look like any eight-year-old boy you might pass in the street.

I've travelled to the ends of the earth and to the centre of the earth. I've been chased by an angry mob of Troglodytes and narrowly avoided being plunged into the earth's molten core! You may think this sounds fantastic; you could think it's a lie. But you would be wrong, because EVERYTHING IN THIS BOOK IS TRUE. Believe this single fact and you can share the most incredible journey ever experienced.

Charlie Small

Attack Of The Ape-men

Fighting for breath, I raced down the dark tunnel that carved its way deeper and deeper into the solid bedrock. Behind me I could hear the heavy footsteps of the razor-toothed ape-man, all hair and solid muscle. I could tell he was gaining on me . . . fast!

My torch showed the tunnel stretching ahead of me into the distant gloom. There was no way of escape and nowhere to hide. What was I going to do? *Help!*

'*Man-cha!*' bellowed the Neanderthal ape-man, and I gasped, because it was a word I sort of recognized. It was like a word I had learned in Gorilla City; just maybe, I thought, these ape-like people spoke a similar language. '*Cha*' was the Gorilla word for banana, and from the horrible slobbery noises this creature was making, I reckoned that '*Man-cha*' must mean 'Man-banana', or 'Man-food'! *Crikey, he wanted me for a snack!*

'*Man-cha!*' he yelled again, and suddenly the tunnel was filled with a hundred voices, all shouting the same thing.

'*Man-cha, man-cha, man-cha!*' A horde of ape-people had joined in the chase. It was turning into a horrific sort of foxhunt – and I was the fox!

I careered down the tunnel, the creature now only a few steps behind, and waited for the tug on my shoulder as his large hairy hand grabbed me. Then, just a few metres further along, a huge rat-like animal shot out of a hole in the wall. It was as big as a badger and ran straight through my legs, into the path of the ape-man.

A rat-like animal, as big as a badger.

'*Man-cha!*' he bellowed again, and fell upon the hapless creature. It squealed and struggled and the ape-man roared and lifted it to his mouth. I couldn't bear to watch what happened next; nor did I have time to. I jumped feet first, straight into the hole from which the rat had just emerged. It was a tight fit, but I managed to wriggle myself in.

Peering out of the narrow burrow, I looked back down the tunnel at a scene of complete mayhem. The rest of the tribe had caught up with my pursuer, seen that he'd got some food and attacked en masse. They must have been starving, because they fought ferociously over the tiniest scraps, roaring and biting and gnashing their teeth.

A Very Close Shave

I felt sorry for the rat. It didn't stand a chance; but I was relieved that it wasn't me being fought over by the mob of hairy thugs. Then I sneezed! An ape-woman heard me and came racing over to the mouth of the burrow. I ducked my head back inside but she thrust her arm in and grabbed a handful of my hair.

'*Yeow!*' I screamed as, twisting and tugging, the creature started to pull me out of the hole like a cork from a bottle. My hunting knife! I needed my hunting knife, but the burrow was too narrow for me to reach round to my rucksack. The ape-woman tugged again and I shot towards the entrance. I was done for!

Then, as I scrabbled on the ground, trying to push myself further back into the burrow, my hand closed on a splinter of stone. Whether it was one of the ape-people's discarded weapons or just a shard of natural flint I don't know, but the edge was razor-sharp and I immediately lifted it to my scalp and sliced through my hair, just below the ape-woman's fist.

This is the shard of stone I used to slice through my hair.

She flew backwards, and I wriggled and writhed deeper into the burrow. Soon her face was back at the entrance and her hand darted in again, but I was out of reach. I let out a huge sigh of relief. The burrow was slightly wider now and I inched back some more, hoping that I would soon be able to sit up.

Soon her face was back at the tunnel entrance

It did get wider – just as the ground started to slope away behind me. I began to slip. I tried to stop but the tunnel got steeper and steeper, and I found myself hurtling backwards into total darkness. *Yikes!*

Down A Slippery Slope

I slid on and on down the dark burrow, happy to be out of the clutches of the ape-people but scared of where I might end up.

Whoa! All of a sudden I shot out and landed in a heap on a hard floor. *Ouch!* Rubbing my bruised bum, I got to my feet and flashed my torch around. I was in a small chamber; ahead of me was the mouth of another tunnel, just like the one I had been chased along. *Oh, marvellous!* I slumped to the floor. Nothing seems to be going right. As soon as I think I'm getting somewhere, I end up slap-bang in the middle of another sticky situation.

Still, I wanted to go exploring; I wanted excitement and I was certainly getting plenty of that! *So, stop snivelling, Charlie Small, and make the most of it*, I said to myself. Things could be worse; I could be behind my desk at St Beckham's doing double maths. Instead, I'm trapped miles underground, in the middle of an amazing adventure.

I must get moving. Sitting in a cave on my backside is not going to find me a way out of here; but first, by the light of my trusty torch, I want to check my explorer's kit and write up my journal.

Taking A Breather

Good! I didn't lose anything out of my rucksack when I was escaping from the antagonistic ape-man. This is what I have in my explorer's kit at the moment:

1) My multi-tooled penknife
2) A ball of string
3) A water bottle (getting dangerously low)
4) A telescope
5) A scarf (I don't know how useful this will be now it's got a large bullet hole through the middle!)
6) An old railway ticket (I found this in a drawer at home and so far I haven't found a train I can use it on)
7) This journal
8) A pack of wild animal collectors cards (really useful)

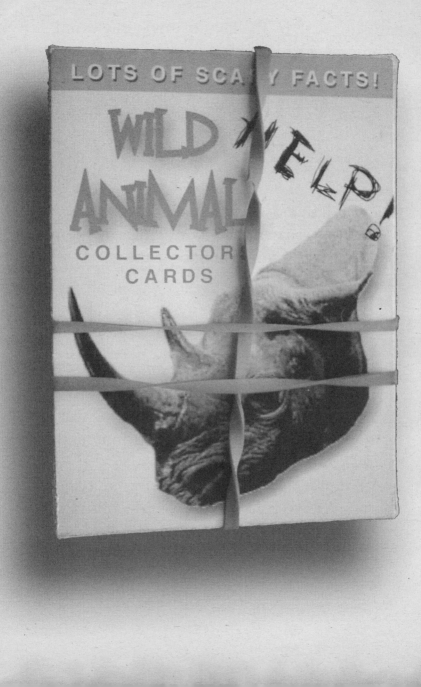

9) A glue pen (to stick any interesting finds in my book)

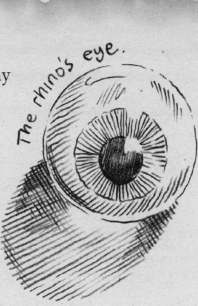

The rhino's eye.

10) A glass eye (my prize possession and a reminder of the bravest friend I have met on my travels so far: the steam-powered rhinoceros)

11) The hunting knife, compass and torch I found on the sun-bleached skeleton of a lost explorer

12) The tooth of a monstrous river crocodile

Life size drawing

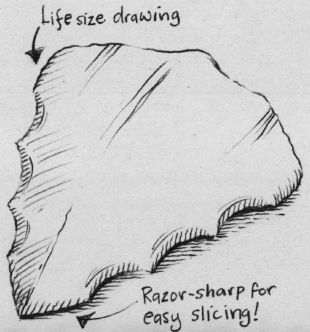

Razor-sharp for easy slicing!

13) A magnifying glass
14) A radio
15) My mobile phone with
wind-up charger
16) The skull of a
Barbarous Bat
17) A bundle of
maps, collected during
my travels
18) A few doubloons from the *Betty Mae*
19) A bag of marbles
20) A large slab of Granny Green's toffee, a bit
melted but still delicious
21) A plastic lemon full of lemon juice
(this proved really useful against a revolting
rattlesnake I met in the Wild, Wild West)
22) The lasso given to me by Wild Bob Ffrance
23) A diamond the size of a walnut. Chief
Sitting Pretty presented it to me for helping save
his son, Nagachak, from Mapwai, the Great Bird
of Death. It's so precious I keep it on a leather
string around my neck!

I'm so glad I brought my explorer's kit with
me. It has saved me loads of times. If you ever
decide to go on a great adventure, make sure

you take one with you. You never know when it might come in handy.

How I Ended up Underground

To think, just this morning I was happily walking across the desert with my friend Jakeman, the inventor. He had just told me *he knew how I could get back home*, when *everything* went wrong!

A huge, hairy hand shot out of the sand, grabbed him by the ankle and dragged him kicking and screaming into the ground! (See my journal, *The Daredevil Desperados of Destiny*!)

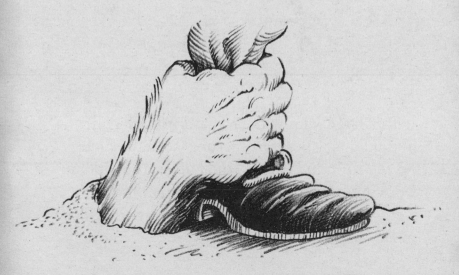

What was going on? I had to do something!
I dug into the sand and found a wide tube
that disappeared into the depths of the earth.
Without thinking, I dived in and slid down into
the blackness. I landed in a narrow tunnel. By
the light of my torch I crept along until I came
to a crack in the tunnel wall. Peering through, I
saw something that set my heart racing!

In a large, dimly lit cave, a horde of half-
human, half-ape-like creatures were breaking
up the rock and carting the pieces away. They
were dressed in moth-eaten animal furs and
were squat, with powerful shoulders and thick,
muscular arms. Their faces were fierce and

heavy-browed; they snarled as they smashed the rocks with their crude tools.

What were they up to? I didn't have time to find out – all of a sudden a great ugly, snag-toothed face was staring straight at me from the other side of the gap. I'd been spotted! With his heavy sledgehammer, the ape-man broke through the tunnel wall between us; I ran!

Soon I was being chased by the whole pack, until I managed to escape down the rat hole and ended up here; I'd lost a lot of my hair, but I still had my head!

Talk about a bad hair day!

Now it's time to find Jakeman. Was he grabbed by one of those hairy apes for dinner, or was it some other hideous creature that dragged him down into this terrible place? I have no idea, but I'm determined to find out . . .

Swamped

I made my way along the tunnel. It was very quiet and I started to feel a bit lonely, so I hummed one of the Daredevil Desperados' campfire songs to keep my spirits up. At least there don't seem to be any ape-men down here, or any more of those revolting rats – or so I thought.

All of a sudden I heard a noise, a strange whooshing sort of sound, and I stopped, straining my ears to listen. The noise got louder and louder; it sounded like water, and it was coming straight towards me! Oh no, don't say the tunnels are flooded. If I were hit by a flood wave, I'd be pounded against the rocks like a rag doll. I turned to run, but I was too late.

Whoosh! Out of the gloom it came, rushing over the rocky floor straight towards me. But it wasn't a river of water. It was a torrent of writhing, wriggling rats; thousands of them, all as big as the one the ape-man had feasted on. I threw myself to the ground, rolling into a ball and holding my breath, as wave after wave of horrendous and humungous fat black rats

Oh rats!

swarmed over me and continued on down the tunnel.

I could feel their sharp claws through my hoodie; I could feel the swish of their scaly tales, and the tunnel was filled with their shrill, ear-piercing squeals. It was disgusting, and there was nothing I could do but wait until they had passed.

Into The Dark

Picking myself up and brushing myself down with a shudder, I carried on down the tunnel. After a while it started to spiral deeper and deeper into the earth. I didn't like the idea of this, but there was no way back and I had no choice but to go wherever the tunnel took me. The air grew stuffier and warmer the deeper I went. *Phew!* It was starting to get really hot. I took off my hoodie and put it in my rucksack.

I started to panic. What if this tunnel didn't lead anywhere? What if it just carried on down to the earth's molten core and I was frazzled like a rasher of bacon? What if I couldn't find a way out of this subterranean sauna and had to wander through these dark tunnels for ever?

Calm down, I told myself. *The worst thing you can do is panic. Take a deep breath. Things could be worse; at least you've got your torch. Imagine how scary it would be if it was completely dark!* It was then that the light started to dim. It was a wind-up torch, so I grabbed the handle and turned it. With a ping, the winder came off in my hand! Oh heck, what was I going to do now?

I shook the torch and for a moment the beam grew brighter; then it dimmed to a faint glow . . . and then it went out completely. The tunnel was pitch black; I couldn't see a thing!

Oh no – it's all gone dark!

The First Sign Of MADNESS!

I wouldn't say I was scared of the dark. I don't need a nightlight in my bedroom or anything (although I do like the landing light on and there's a streetlamp outside our house that shines through my bedroom window), but now I was in *complete* darkness, and I didn't like it one little bit. Just try putting your head under the bedcovers when all the lights are off. Dark, isn't it? Well, this was even darker!

The tunnel was pitch black!

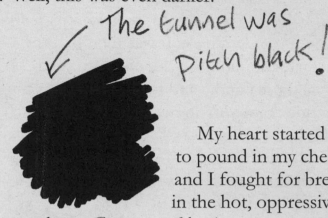

My heart started to pound in my chest and I fought for breath in the hot, oppressive atmosphere. *Get me out of here!*

'Help!' I yelled, and my voice echoed away down the tunnel and disappeared into silence. 'Help! Help!'

Then, 'Stop it, Charlie Small,' I said out loud. 'What are you, a boy or a mouse? You're four hundred years old, for goodness' sake. Some intrepid explorer you are if you can't stand the dark. Pull yourself together!' And just to make sure I was paying attention I gave myself a slap on the face.

'Ouch! That hurt,' I said.

'Good,' I replied. 'Let that be a lesson to you; any more whining and I'll dish out another.'

'OK, sorry,' I said, taking a deep breath and calming down. 'I'm feeling much better now. There's one more thing, though.'

'What?'

'You really must stop talking to yourself. Anyone would think you'd gone bonkers!'

Have I gone bonkers?!

The Buzz!

I don't know how long I spent shuffling along in the dark – an hour? a day maybe? – but then I thought I heard a noise. *Not more rats*, I prayed. I stopped walking and held my breath.

Yes, there was definitely a low buzzing noise ahead, like an electric generator. I crept forward silently, and as the tunnel turned, I realized I could see the walls. Only faintly, but I could definitely make out some rocky lumps and bumps.

As I kept going, the hum grew louder *BZzZZzZ!*

and the light grew brighter, and suddenly, just ahead, I saw an intense golden glow coming from a hole in the wall, lighting up a long stretch of the tunnel.

Busy Little Bees

While I watched, a cluster of little golden globes of light floated out of the hole, hung in the air for a moment and then shot off down the tunnel. As they did so, some more passed them coming the other way. Humming loudly, they bustled around the entrance to the hole and then disappeared inside.

Almost immediately another group of floating lights emerged from the rock and I understood what I was seeing. They were insects. Strange, glowing insects returning to their nest. I had heard of glow-worms of course, but these were so much bigger. They were about the size of a tennis ball, with little corkscrew tails; they glowed bright yellow . . . *and they gave me an idea!*

The strange
glow bug thing!

A Flying Torch!

I crept up to the hole and peered inside. It was so bright I had to squint, but when my eyes had got used to the glare I could make out a swarm of insects crawling over the surface of the rock, which they had drilled full of holes with their corkscrew tails.

Dipping into my rucksack, I took out the glue pen; with my multi-tooled penknife I cut a two-metre length from my ball of string; then, reaching into the hole and praying that the bugs weren't poisonous, I carefully closed my hand around one and lifted it out.

Whoa! – the bug didn't sting, but vibrated so hard in my hand that it sent a tingling sensation right up my arm! Carefully, I let one of its black, feathery legs poke out between my fingers and dabbed on a spot of glue. I touched one end of the string against the glue spot, held it for a few seconds and then let the creature go. It buzzed

My own flying torch!

into the air on the end of the string, and I tied the other end around my wrist.

Brilliant, it worked – I had my own flying torch! Now I could see where I was going, I raced down the tunnel, determined to find a way out as quickly as possible. The insect followed on its lead a metre or so above my head, lighting my way with a warm yellow light.

A Pillar Of Strength!

Oh boy, was I glad I'd found my bug light because suddenly I came to a spot where the floor of the tunnel had collapsed. All that remained was a series of narrow columns about two metres apart, just like this:

The floor had collapsed, leaving a series of narrow columns!

If I'd still been in the dark, I would have fallen straight between the columns and been dashed onto the jagged rocks below.

There was nothing for it but to jump from one pillar to the next. I sprang into the air, landing on top of the first one and waving my arms around like a windmill to try and keep my balance. *Phew!* This was going to be tricky! Panting with effort, I jumped again and again, dislodging cascades of stones that rattled down to the rocks below.

Some of the pillars were only about ten centimetres wide, and once I very nearly fell. It was only with the help of the insect tied to my wrist that I managed to regain my balance. As I started to fall backwards, it flapped its tiny wings so fast they buzzed like an outboard motor, and it managed to hold me upright until I found my footing. Thanks, bug!

A Tight Spot

At last I reached solid ground again and continued on my way. The tunnel went on and on, and the ceiling got lower and lower. Soon I had to crawl along on all fours. This was no fun at all and I was glad to have my friendly bug for company.

I began to feel very hungry; it was ages since I'd eaten anything, but the only food I had in my rucksack was the large slab of toffee that Granny Green had given me after I defeated the evil Puppet Master. That would have to do. I ripped off the wrapper and took a huge bite.

Mmmm! Delicious – and I wasn't the only one to think so, because the glow bug dived onto the toffee and started sucking away with its weird pointy mouth. In fact it loved it so much I had to prise it away and quickly wrap up the toffee before it scoffed the lot!

'We must leave some for later,' I said. 'Now let's see where this tiny passage leads.'

Soon the tunnel was so small I had to slide along on my tummy. Then, all at once, a faint smell like bad eggs wafted along the narrow passageway. Where was it coming from? I squeezed through a tiny gap between two protruding rocks and stepped into a large underground chamber.

The glow bug was a real greedy guts.

Help! I was worried I would get stuck in the tiny tunnel.

The Real Pits

In the floor ahead of me was a deep pit that glowed with an intense red light. It stretched right across the cavern, so although I could see the entrance to a large tunnel on the far side, I couldn't reach it. My way was barred.

Every few seconds, with a bubbling, belching sound, great clouds of steam billowed from the depths of the pit and floated up to the ceiling. Now the bad egg smell was really strong; it stung my nostrils and made my throat feel dry and sore. Stepping towards the crater, I could see a fiery river of thick molten lava passing through a wide fracture in the rock, hundreds of metres below. There must be a way across, I said to myself, and looking up, I saw something that gave me an idea . . . But just as I reached for my lasso I heard a shuffling noise behind me.

I spun round. *Oh no!* Standing at the entrance to another tunnel was the ape-man.

'*Man-cha!*' he bellowed.

Yikes. Get me out of here!

A Tarzan-like Escape!

I ran, dragging the glow bug behind me and unfurling my lasso at the same time. The ape-man followed hot on my heels. I twirled my lasso once, twice, three times, and threw it up towards the ceiling.

With a satisfying *thunk* the loop tightened around a projecting rock, and I launched myself into a running jump. I soared over the deep, bubbling pit, and as I looked back at the ape-man, who was now standing at the edge of the crater with a very confused look on his face, I let out a Tarzan-like yell of triumph.

'*Aah-aah-aah-aah-aah!*'

And then the rock snapped off. I dropped my lasso and tumbled head over heels into the fiery pit below!

Out Of The Frying Pan And Into The Fire!

I plummeted down, the air scorching me as I fell towards the pool of lava below. *Yikes!*

Then, all of a sudden, I stopped in mid-air!

It sounds impossible, I know, but it's true: I was suspended halfway down with the face of the stupid ape-man peering at me from above and the river of liquid rock writhing and boiling below. *What's going on?* I wondered, feeling all around me. Then I realized what had happened – I was caught in a net!

The strings of the net were so fine they were almost invisible, but they were very strong, and sticky, and stretched right across the pit. But who would bother putting a net in such a strange place, and what was it for?

It was then that I saw a grisly sight: caught in the net at my feet and staring up at me with a terrible toothy grin was a human skull. *Oh yikes!* Someone else had fallen down here, and been unable to climb out. What a terrible end! I felt the searing heat of the molten lava below and knew I would have to get out pretty quick myself, or I would start to cook through like a burger on a barbecue. I studied the rock face, trying to find an escape route. Yes, there was a way up: with the help of my explorer's kit I was sure I could climb out.

As I scrambled across the mesh towards the rock wall, I realized that the netting was littered

Wow! It's so hot down here

A grinning skull stared up at me!

with skulls and leg bones and ribcages. *Yuck!
How revolting!* But surely not all of these scalded
skeletons had been unable to escape. What on
earth had happened to them?

Then I felt the net start to vibrate. It wasn't
me making the strings quiver and pulse;
something else was moving across it! I looked
around and my heart leaped into my throat:
crawling straight towards me was the ugliest,
scariest, most vicious-looking insect I have ever
seen, and this one was way too big to squash
between the pages of my journal!

Spidion Attack - HELP!

It was a revolting, creeping-crawling, monstrous fat spider, as big as an armchair. The web bowed under the creature's weight as it waved a deadly three-pronged tail, which curved over its back like a scorpion's.

The deep purple hairs on the creature's body waved in the updraught from the hot pit. Its tail and forelegs were a dirty lemon yellow and covered with a smooth, hard carapace. Scared as I was, the explorer side of me was fascinated. I was sure this was another new species to add to my list and I immediately called it the Spidion!

Uh-oh! After pausing and testing the scorching air with its front legs, the infernal insect scuttled straight towards me. Its bony forelegs clattered like knives; it hissed like a punctured tyre and dribbled a continuous stream of thick, custard-like liquid from between its jaws. Disgusting!

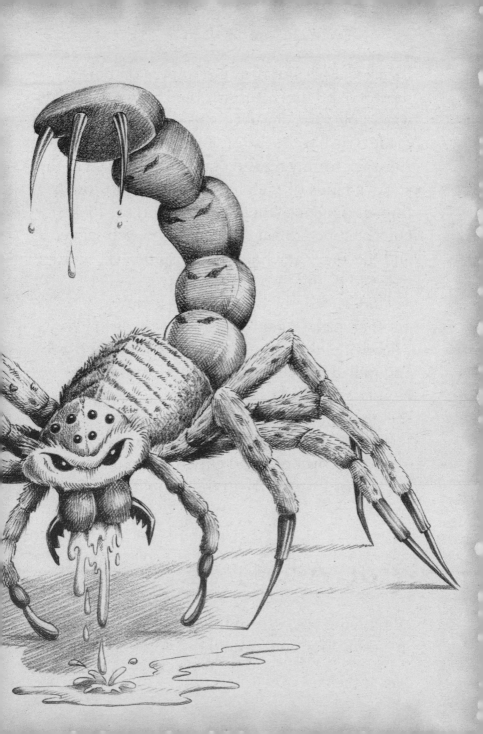

I backed away, but the Spidion was on home territory and much surer-footed than me. How was I going to get out of this? As the Spidion made a rush towards me, I felt around in my rucksack for my hunting knife and slashed at the sticky strands of web in front of it. The tough threads pinged as they snapped and the loose ends whipped through the air. The web sagged and the angry arachnid had to step back in order to avoid falling through the tear.

Undeterred, the Spidion attacked from another angle. Again I slashed at the web. Now *I* nearly fell through the hole: I grabbed the web and pulled myself back up, enveloped in the cloud of steaming sulphur that belched up from the deep pit. The Spidion moved again and I realized that if I didn't do something fast, I would be cornered, and either the animal would get me, or I would fry in the bubbling river below.

Cut And Run

Wiping the sweat from my forehead, I set off in a crouching run around the Spidion, my feet now finding the tiny threads with ease. It must have been all the training I did up in the rigging of the pirate ship.

I kept slicing at the web with my knife and it started to give way in the middle. The Spidion

followed me, dribbling and gurgling, the deadly tail whipping through the air and stabbing at me with its scimitar-like stings. As I neared the far wall of the crater, the web around my attacker sagged more and more; finally it gave way completely. Scrabbling wildly to try and regain its footing, the Spidion gave an ear-splitting screech and started to fall.

'Yes, got you!' I cried in relief; but it wasn't over yet!

The Spidion dived towards me, grabbing a single strand of web with one of its legs and pulling itself back up. I lunged forward to try and cut the web, but with another screech the insect squirted a stream of thick, custardy spit straight into my face. I wiped away the revolting gunge just as its huge tail whipped towards me, the deadly stingers aiming straight for my back.

Still half blind, I stabbed at the web and dived out of the way; but I had only managed to cut halfway through it.

'*Weeaark!*' the animal cried, its legs flailing wildly in the air as its tail stabbed at me – once, twice – both blows glancing off my trusty old rucksack. The blows must have loosened the flap because, out of the corner of my eye, I saw my precious crocodile's tooth and my telescope drop into the steaming pit.

Then, with a loud *twang*, the tough little thread snapped and the Spidion fell screaming towards the boiling magma below. The heat must be unbelievable down there: way before it reached the raging river, the Spidion evaporated into thin air.

The spidion evaporated into thin air!

BOOF!

Stuck In The Pit

I scrambled away from the torn edge of the web
and sat with my back against the hot side of the
pit. With my heart banging away in my chest
like a steam hammer, I realized I was starting
to cook and decided to waste no time in getting
out of the sulphurous chasm.

I began to climb, following the route I had roughly mapped out in my mind. All I had to do was get onto an overhang some thirty metres above my head, and from there I could lasso another projection and climb the rope to the top. There was just one problem with this plan. Correction, there were just two problems with this plan:

1) I couldn't climb up the side of the pit. It was covered with a weird kind of greasy, sticky moss, which, as soon as I touched it, excreted a soapy gunk that made climbing impossible.

2) Even if I could get up to the platform, I couldn't use my lasso. I've just remembered, I dropped it! It must have fallen into the fiery pit and burned to a frazzle. Oh blow and double darn it! This is really, *really* bad news – the lasso was one of the most important things in my explorer's kit. I'll have to get a replacement, and soon!

SO, I WAS TRAPPED IN A BUBBLING CRATER WITH A RIVER OF FIRE BELOW AND AN ANGRY APE-MAN ABOVE!

Yes, he was still there, looking down in his gormless way.

'*Man-cha!*' he yelled, and raised his long, hairy arms above his head.

'*Man-cha* to you too!' I bellowed back. 'Now shut up, I'm trying to think.' I sat down again and looked through my explorer's kit, hoping to find something that might help me escape.

Man-cha to you too!

What Now?

As I did so, the glow bug that was still attached to my wrist started buzzing about frantically. Poor thing – I had forgotten all about it. It must have been thrown about like a rag doll during my fight with the Spidion. The kindest thing to do would be to let it go. The glow from the molten lava below gave me more than enough light to see by, and if I ever managed to get out of the pit and found myself in the dark again, I would just have to deal with it as best I could.

I snipped through the string with my knife and the glow bug buzzed noisily away. As soon as my little friend had gone, I tried scaling the rock wall again. Desperately, I scrabbled and scrambled and clambered and climbed, but it was way too slimy. As soon as I thought I was getting somewhere, I slid right back down onto the web again.

'Darn it!' I cried angrily. By now,

My bug buzzed off

I was getting really hot – in fact my clothes were starting to smoke! I looked up towards the ape-man. 'Can't you throw down a rope or something, you hairy, ham-fisted hulk?' But he was no longer there; I was totally on my own.

Oh no! What am I going to do? How am I . . . ? Hold on, what's that buzzing noise?

The Light Flight

The buzzing grew louder and louder. Over the rim of the pit far above my head came a whole swarm of glow bugs. The one in the lead had a piece of string still dangling from its back leg, and I realized it must be my little yellow friend. The insects swarmed together above my head in one shifting ball of light. My pet bug flew down to my wrist and then up to the swarm again. What did it mean?

Then, as it repeated its actions, I understood. I quickly unrolled the ball of string from my rucksack, cutting off equal lengths until I had as many bits of string as there were insects. I dabbed a blob of glue onto the end of

each string and held it up.
Immediately, a bug flew
down, dipped a leg into
the paste and then
rejoined its friends in the
swarm.

Before long, a cloud of
insects as large as a beach
ball glowed brilliantly above
my head. From below them
hung a festoon of strings, which
I grabbed hold of. The humming
increased and the bugs flew up,
lifting me effortlessly into the air.
I held on tight – very tight: one
slip and I would be sizzling in
the lava like a sausage. *Go, bugs,
go!*

On Solid Ground – But In A Tight Spot

Yahoo, yee-hah, yippee! and all the other cowboy cries I can think of. We made it! The friendly insects lifted me clean out of the pit and dropped me gently at the mouth of the tunnel I had been trying to reach in the first place. Why on earth did they help? What could they want in return? Then, as soon as I let them go, I knew exactly what they wanted!

They swarmed, humming and buzzing, around my rucksack, as excited as puppies over a bone. It was the toffee – Granny Green's toffee, which I had given my bug for breakfast. They were crazy for it, and if I hadn't opened the flap and taken out the slab of toffee right away, I think they would have burrowed straight through the canvas to get to it!

I held the toffee out towards the mad swarm of insects, which were lighting the tunnel as brightly as the sun. I turned to see if there was any sign of the ape-man, but the far side of the pit was still deserted. He had probably gone back down the tunnel to his tribe. Good! That was one less thing to worry about.

But oh no! When I turned back again, the massive man-monster was standing right in front of me. Uh! How on earth did he get there? Then I saw the entrance to a side tunnel. *Oh, that's great*, I thought. There must be a passage leading all the way round the pit from the chamber. I needn't have tried swinging over it in the first place. But never mind about that. What was I going to do with the lump of muscle standing in front of me?

In The Grip Of The Ape-man

I couldn't go back because of the fiery pit, and
I couldn't go forward because of the ape-man.
I WAS TRAPPED!

Then my friendly insects swarmed towards
the great hairy creature, darting around his head,
trying to distract him. As the big ape staggered
about, swiping them away, a narrow gap opened
between him and the passage wall and I went
for it.

Crouching low, I barged my way past the
nutty Neanderthal. I thought I'd made it, but
then I felt his huge hand grab me by the scruff
of the neck. I dropped the toffee and the insects
pounced on it as the ape-man lifted me clean
off the ground.

Nose to nose, we stared each other in the
face. The ape-man gave a grin, licked his
lips and chuckled. It sounded like someone
stamping along a wet gravel path.

'*Man-cha*,' he said, and then to my utter
amazement he put me back on the ground, took
my hand in his massive hairy paw and led me
down the tunnel as if I were a toddler and we
were out for a stroll in the park!

Walking With The Ape-man

I didn't know what was going on, but I didn't want to be in the hands of this great hairy brute, so I pulled and I tugged and I dug my heels into the rock-strewn floor of the tunnel. But it was no good; I couldn't pull free.

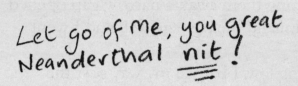

Let go of me, you great Neanderthal <u>nit</u>!

In fact I don't think the ape-man even noticed I was struggling. He just led me casually down the passage, turning every now and then to grunt '*Man-cha*' at me, snuffling like a great grizzly bear.

Man-cha, man-cha, man-cha – was that the only thing he could say? And if it did mean 'man-banana', why wasn't I already stewing in the juices of his great pot belly?

Does Man-cha mean Man-banana?

A Light At The End Of The Tunnel

Soon I became aware of a faint glow in the distance. *Oh, not another pit!* I thought. Then, as we turned a bend in the passage, a brilliant white light hit me. I screwed up my eyes, shielding them with my free hand.

The light was strange; it was as bright as day, but somehow I knew we were nowhere near the daylight. It had an odd bluish tinge, more like moonlight than sunshine, but brighter.

'*Wow!*' I cried in amazement as we stepped out of the tunnel.

The Great Cavern

We were still underground, but had emerged into an immense cavern. The walls beside me arced hundreds of metres above my head, disappearing into an intense brightness. How weird; it was as if the light came from the rock itself. Glancing at the granite wall by my side, I realized this was *exactly* where it came from!

The cavern wall was covered with a filigree

of white opalescent veins that gave a powerful glow; where the veins were thickest, the light was stronger. It was fantastic, and looking around in awe, I slowly became aware of the vastness of the cavern I was in.

The walls stretched out on either side of me, disappearing into the distance; to my left were the foothills of some gigantic underground mountain range; scattered all around were great milky-white columns; a hundred metres or so in front of me was the shore of a huge, placid underground lake, so large it stretched all the way to the horizon. It was incredible!

The ape-man pulled me forward, leading me down to the water's edge, where a dilapidated wooden jetty stretched out into the lake. I had

given up struggling by now;
there was no point. The mountain
of muscle sat me down on the jetty
and looked out across the black water.

'*Man-cha*,' he grunted, pointing at me. What
on earth did he mean? What was he showing
me? He repeated his actions and then, fumbling
amongst the coarse hairy garments he wore, he
pulled out a package and placed it on the jetty
beside me. Then he looked pleadingly into my
eyes, turned on his heel and walked back to
the mouth of the tunnel. Without a backward
glance, he disappeared inside.

What was all that about?

A Light Snack

Now I was totally confused. One minute I was expecting to be pulverized by the Neolithic ape-man's stone sledgehammer, cracked in half across his hairy knees and then eaten; the next minute the numbskull had sat me down, given me a parcel and left me on an old jetty by the side of a huge black lake. What was I supposed to do now?

First things first – find out what's in the parcel! I had only removed the top layer of grubby wrapping when the smell told me it was food, and my tummy gurgled in anticipation. I was absolutely starving; apart from the toffee, I hadn't eaten for ages. I unwrapped it further. Oh yum! It was a sandwich, a doorstep of thick, crusty bread with a filling that smelled so tasty.

It was only after I had sunk my teeth deep into the sarnie that I noticed the thick, scaly tail poking out. *Ugh!* I spat the mouthful onto the floor and tentatively pulled the two slices of bread apart. Inside was a rat, a revolting fat rat, just like the one in the tunnel. It had been squashed and compressed into a sort of pâté, sure, but it was still unmistakably a rat!

My Sandwich

Rat pâté – you've got to be kidding!

My stomach turned over, and I thought I was going to puke, but then the smell hit me again. It smelled really, really good – and I was very, very hungry. I closed my eyes and opened my mouth to take another bite . . .

You don't need to hear any more about my snack – all you need to know is I'm no longer hungry!

Waiting For The Ferryman

For the last hour I've been writing up my latest adventures in this journal, trying to jot everything down while it's still fresh in my mind. I think that's the lot. So, what shall I do now?

Well, I may not be hungry any more, but I *am* tired. In fact, after my desperate fight with the Spidion, I am exhausted, so I'm going to lie down on the jetty for a proper rest. Hold on, what's this? I've been leaning against a signpost all the time. The letters on the board are worn and cracked, but I can just make them out:

FERRY TO SUBTERRANEA

Times: Whenever Possible
— (I go as fast as I can)

Price: Depends how big you are, how heavy you are, and how rich you are!
WAIT HERE ↓

Is that what the ape-man was telling me — to take the ferry to Subterranea? Is that where Jakeman is? Well, I don't have anything else to do and I certainly don't want to go back into the tunnels, so I might as well wait. Looking across the water, I can't see any sign of a ferry, so I'm going to curl up on the ground and get some sleep.

Waiting Some More!

I don't know how long I slept; it's impossible to judge the passing of time in this permanently bright cavern.

There is still no sign of a ferry anywhere on the water.

Still Waiting...

No ferry yet – maybe they've stopped the service. Getting bored.

Later

Getting really bored!

Hurry up!

I'm tired of waiting
Don't get caught in the Spidion's We
Man-cha!
One of the tricky troublesome Ape-men
Where is the ferryman?

Ape-men
are trouble. TRUE!
get me a spade
I am getting boRed
New, delicious
Sandwich filling
light
bug
Spidion
Custardy
Spit!
You dirty
rat!
I see
lots of
these!

Much Later

He's coming! The ferryman is coming. I can see a small dot on the horizon. It won't be long now.

Much, Much Later!

Come on – hurry up!

This underground lake must be huge, because the tiny dot has been on the horizon for ages and never seems to get any nearer; but at last the figure *is* getting closer. I can hear the slap of the ferryman's paddle – and now he's calling out. His voice sounds strange in the massive cavern, echoing across the smooth black water.

'Whoever awaits ferryman have correct fare ready. Form an orderly queue,' he cries in a flat, vacant voice.

Form an orderly queue? I'm the only person here, and judging by the state of the jetty, I'm the only person who's been here for ages!

Now, without the slightest of splashes, the ferryman is mooring his flat-bottomed punt to the jetty, and I can take a proper look at him.

Wow! What a weird little man!

Whoops! I've just realized – I don't think I've got any money for the fare. Will he let me travel for nothing? I *must* get across the dark waters and find news of Jakeman.

I have to stop writing now and try and wheedle a free ride.

What Happened?

The next thing I remember, I was waking from a deep and dreamless sleep. I felt as if I'd been snoozing for a hundred years, just like that girl in the fairy tale.

I opened my eyes and gasped. I was lying on a strange bed in a gloomy room. Somewhere beyond the pool of light cast by a small window, I could hear something shuffling about. Panicking, I sat up quickly and *oooh!* my head throbbed – it was wrapped in a thick bandage. What was going on? Where was I? How did I get here?

The shuffling noise stopped. There was complete silence. Then it started again and I

Where am I?

realized it was getting closer and closer. Wide-eyed, I stared into the dark, waiting for whatever it was to emerge from the shadows.

'Oh good, you've decided to wake up!' said a friendly voice, and a lady stepped into the light.

Again I gasped. 'Mum?' I said. 'Is that you? Am I home?' For a second I thought that my adventures had just been a dream. I must have had an accident – a bump on the head – and imagined it all. Now I'd woken up in my own bed and everything was going to be OK.

'Oh no, dear,' said the lady, chuckling, 'I'm not your mum. Drink this,' she said, placing a glass of water on the little bedside table. Now I could see she was nothing like my mum; she was a short, round lady with wrinkly grey skin! But she reminded me of someone. Oh, I know – the ferryman! I had forgotten all about him.

'Where am I?' I said, trying to get out of bed.

The little round, mud-coloured lady.

60

'You stay right there,' said the lady. 'You've had a nasty bump on the head. I don't know how you got it, but I found you unconscious on the seashore.'

'My explorer's kit!' I cried. 'Where's my rucksack?'

'Don't worry, it's safe,' the kind lady told me, dragging my rucksack from under the bed. 'You were also holding this in your hand. I don't know if it means anything to you . . .' She felt in the pocket of her pinny and pulled out a fang that made my river croc's tooth look like a baby's! It was massive, ginormous! And as soon as I saw it, the whole scary, dangerous, crazy, catastrophic journey across the Wide Subterrestrial Sea came flooding back.

← sharp as a needle.

Deadly barbs! →

The Mega-tooth! Imagine being gnawed by a mouthful of these!

This Is What Happened

The ferryman arrived at the little jetty, and I don't think I've ever seen a stranger-looking man. He was small and skinny with a large round head, a tiny nose and a wrinkled face. The weirdest thing about him was the grey, muddy colour of his skin. This is what the ferryman looked like:

'You go to Subterranea?' he asked in a voice that bubbled like a bilious swamp.

'I suppose I do,' I said, not really sure where or what Subterranea was. 'Is it very far?'

'Twenty tulsa,' gurgled the man, holding out his hand.

'Not how much, how far?' I asked.

'Yes, how far!' said the mud-man. 'Twenty tulsa!'

I sighed, patting my pockets. 'I don't seem to have any cash on me,' I said, 'but it's really, really important that I get away from here. *It could be a matter of life and death.*'

'Goodbye!' said the ferryman, lifting his long oar.

'No, wait! I must have something here that will do,' and I tipped up my rucksack, letting its contents spill onto the wooden jetty. The ferryman was out of his boat in an instant, sorting through my explorer's kit and quickly dividing the contents into three neat piles.

'Maybe; rubbish; big load of rubbish,' he said, pointing at each pile in turn. 'What else you got? Something shiny – I like shiny.'

'Nothing,' I said, trying to hide the walnut-sized diamond that Chief Sitting Pretty had given me, which was hanging round my neck.

'Goodbye,' said the ferryman again.

'Wait!' I cried, just about to untie the leather thong that held the precious diamond, but as I did so, something else caught the ferryman's eye. He pounced on my rucksack, thrusting his hand to the bottom and pulling out one of the doubloons I had managed to save from my time aboard Captain Cut-throat's ship, the *Betty Mae*.

'You hide – you hide shiny,' he said accusingly.

'You hide shiny'

'No, not at all,' I said. 'It must have got stuck in the stitching at the bottom of my bag. You keep it. It must be worth a hundred tulsas!'

'Million tulsas!' said the ferryman, chuckling
with delight and polishing the doubloon on his
muddy sleeve. He quickly climbed back aboard
his flat-bottomed boat and beckoned to me,
thrusting his oar into the water at the same time.
I just had time to gather my stuff together, and
running full pelt along the jetty, I leaped onto
the boat as it floated out onto the black lake.

Across The Water

With long, languorous strokes the ferryman
sent the punt slapping across the surface of the
water. He stood silently at the back of the boat,
looking towards the horizon. I tried to talk to
him – there were so many questions I wanted to
ask – but the muddy little man ignored me, so in
the end I gave up.

We drifted for hours, the intense silence
broken only by the slap of the paddle on the
water. A mist started to form, and before long
the air was as thick and white as milk. There was
no way the ferryman could see where he was
going, but he confidently paddled on, navigating
by instinct and experience.

All of a sudden a huge shadowy shape broke
through the mist in front of us. The ferryman
dug his oar into the water, steering us alongside
the mysterious object. Then a slight breeze
shifted the mist and I could see what had nearly
run us down: a galleon, or rather the rotted hulk
of a galleon. Its hull was full of holes, exposing
a skeleton of beams and struts; the sails hung in
tatters from the yardarms.

'Whoa!' I yelled.

'What?' barked the ferryman.

'Stop!' I cried. 'Please, just for a minute.' I had
seen something that made my blood run cold.

My Old Home!

On the bows of the ship hung a sign, its chipped lettering spelling out the name *Betty Mae*. It was Captain Cut-throat's pirate galleon, the ship I had lived on for such a long time; the ship where I had made so many good friends and such terrible enemies. But why was she in such a sorry state and how on earth did she end up thousands of metres below ground?

As the ferryman held the punt steady, I took a huge leap, grabbing hold of a beam on the *Betty Mae*'s hull. Quickly and quietly, I climbed up to the rotting main deck. It was deserted.

'Wait there,' I called down to the ferryman. 'I won't be long.' I went down the steps to the captain's cabin. This too was deserted, although the ship's charts, Cut-throat's chest of clothes and her collection of scrimshawed whale's teeth were where they had always been. It was so strange – like being on a stage set with no actors. I expected Cut-throat or Rawcliffe Annie to come crashing down the steps at any minute, cursing and bawling and calling for rum; but I knew that nobody had been here for a very long time.

What on earth could have happened to make the brave band of female felons desert their beloved home? Perhaps they'd been taken prisoner by Craik, chief thief-taker and all-round no-good dog, after I had made my escape; perhaps they'd teamed up with their pirate husbands aboard the *Saracen's Skull*.
(See my Journal, The Perfumed Pirates of Perfidy)

I would probably never know, but I found it all a bit sad – and very, very creepy; all of a sudden I wanted to get away.

The Betty Mae was just like a ghost ship.

But first things first: 'Once a pirate, always a pirate,' I said to myself, and I heaved open the lid of the *Betty Mae*'s treasure chest, which stood in the corner of the captain's cabin. Darn it – it was empty. No, hold on . . . I reached into the bottom and pulled out a small sack of jingling golden coins. This could come in useful!

The jingling bag of dosh!

In fact it came in useful straight away, because when I returned to the deck and peered down to where I had left the ferryman, there was no one there! I stared into the mist, but I couldn't see a thing. I had been abandoned. Of all the double-crossing villains!

'Hey!' I called out. 'Come back!' Nothing. I tried again, but there was still no reply. Oh, help! 'I've got lots of lovely shiny stuff here!' I bellowed, hoping that if the ferryman was within earshot this might tempt him back. 'I'll share it fifty-fifty with you.'

I was right: almost immediately I heard a faint voice calling through the mist.

'Coming!' A few minutes later the ferryman's punt appeared through the swirling fog. 'Sorry, young master,' he said. 'I must have drifted away in the current.'

'Oh, sure,' I replied, looking down at the still calm of the ocean. 'Of course you did.' I knew then and there that this weird little man was not to be trusted.

I clambered back into the punt, and the greedy ferryman was pulling at the sack of gold before I'd even sat down.

'Clear off,' I warned him. 'I'll give you your share when we land.'

But as it turned out, neither of us was destined to get our share of the booty!

On To Subterranea

Now he knew there was some extra 'shiny' to be had, the ferryman suddenly became much friendlier. It was time to try and get some answers to the questions that had been bothering me.

'Back there, in the labyrinth of tunnels, I was chased by some ape-men. Do you know who they are?' I asked.

'Ape-men?' said the ferryman as he paddled.

'Big hairy brutes with long, muscly arms,' I explained.

'Troglodytes,' said the ferryman. 'Troglodytes from Barbaria.'

'Bad men?' I asked.

The ferryman shrugged his shoulders. 'Some good, some bad.'

'But they kept yelling "*Man-cha.*" I think it means "Man-food"; I think they were going to eat me.'

'Perhaps,' said the ferryman. '*Man-cha* mean "I kill you". It mean "Me friend" and "Hello" and "Help me". It's only word Trogs use. It depend *how* they say it.'

I had been right. *Man-cha was* the only word the Troglodytes used. So, had they been trying to eat me or help me? I wasn't sure any more; perhaps I should have stayed with them – perhaps they weren't man-eating monsters. But it was too late to worry about it now, because we were on our way to some place called Subterranea.

'Where is Subterranea?' I asked.

Tutting loudly at my incessant questions, the ferryman reached under a low bench-seat at the back of the punt. He pulled out a sheaf of papers and handed the top one to me. It was a map . . .

Allotments

Subterranea

Harbour

The Wide
Subterrestrial
Sea

Barbaria

Not to Scale.

... a fantastic map showing some of the tunnels I had crawled through; it showed the water I was sailing on right now, which wasn't a lake at all, but a proper underground ocean; it showed the island called Barbaria, where the ape-men, or Troglodytes, came from; it showed, on the far coast of the huge ocean, a large city called Subterranea.

My heart gave a flutter of excitement. That's where we were heading right now. Would I find Jakeman there? Would the inhabitants be friendly or hostile? Would – *Wow! Blimey, what was that?* The ferryman whimpered as a massive triangular shadow passed over the punt. He pointed over my shoulder, but when I turned round there was nothing there, just a slight ripple disturbing the surface of the calm, cold ocean.

The Megashark!

'What was that?' I asked in a panic. The ferryman didn't reply, but I could see by the look on his face that whatever it was, it wasn't good news.

The sea remained glassy, but quickly took on an ominous look: black and still and threatening. The ferryman was plunging his oar into the water, driving the punt along, looking to the left and right with wide, frightened eyes.

Then, all of a sudden, way over to our left, the ocean was split by a trail of sparkling silver bubbles as a small flat shape broke the surface.

'Oh, help! Save poor ferryman!' cried my petrified companion.

'What is it?' I asked again. The shape grew larger and larger, curving back like a huge scythe until it was as big as the sail on a yacht. I didn't have to ask what it was again. I knew it was the dorsal fin of a shark; a shark so big it could have swallowed my old foe the river crocodile in one mouthful – and the great sail-shaped fin was heading straight towards us!

Split Asunder

CRASH! The fin hit our punt bang in the middle, cutting through it like a buzz saw, and the ferryman and I were left spinning wildly in mid-ocean, each hanging on for dear life in a separate half of the punt.

Icy water slopped around my ankles as I began to sink. I tried to bail out with my hands, but it was no good; the hull disappeared below me and sank to the dark depths of the ocean. In a mad doggy-paddle I floundered about, the weight of my rucksack pulling me down, but I managed to grab hold of a wide plank of wood that had broken away from the punt.

I looked over at the ferryman. Frozen with fear, he cowered in his half of the punt, which was still afloat but sitting very low in the water. There was no sign of the shark fin and I started to kick my legs in an attempt to help him, but I didn't have time: the surface of the sea exploded in an eruption of foam as the massive bulk of the Megashark launched itself into the air in a wide arcing dive. For a few seconds it seemed to hang there, as both the ferryman and I watched in horror. It was huge; as big as a house! Then

Help! Shark!

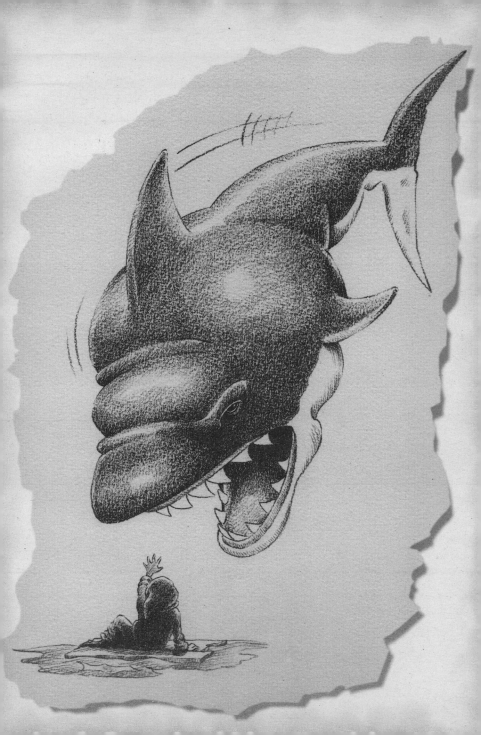

down it came, its massive mouth wide open, displaying row upon row of incredible incisors.

The ferryman raised his arms, but he didn't even have time to cry out. He disappeared into the Megashark's gaping jaw as, with a mighty splash, it dived back into the sea. Frozen with horror, I was almost immediately lifted up on the huge swell of water created by the diving monster.

Up I went, desperately hanging onto my piece of wood as the wave grew and grew. Glancing over my shoulder, I saw the tall fin screaming through the water in my wake.

'*Aaargh!*' I yelled. Then, as I reached the crest of the towering wave, I had an idea. Pulling the plank closer, I managed to slide it underneath my tummy. In a single smooth action, I jumped into a squatting position and stood up, arms extended for balance. I was surfing! I'd never surfed before, and I could think of better ways to learn, but I was managing to stay upright!

With a slight adjustment to my balance, I turned my surfboard until it was skimming along the crest of the wave. Looking down, I realized just how big the wave had grown. I was thirty metres above the surface of the ocean and zipping along at about a hundred kilometres per hour.

Wobbling and nearly losing my balance, I glanced behind me. The Megashark was still there, but it wasn't gaining on me. Quickly shifting my weight, I flipped the board through a hundred and eighty degrees. The shark was slow to react and continued shooting along in the opposite direction. I now had some breathing space and could concentrate on my surfing. I needed to!

As the wave started to break, my speed increased. I was going so fast I was finding it hard to take a breath. Then the crest curved over my head and I was shooting through a tunnel of silver water, my ears filled with the roar of the wave. I was beginning to enjoy myself, but it didn't last long. Out of the corner of my eye I could see the silhouette of the Megashark tracking me from inside the wave. It had caught up with me again!

Suddenly the shark's enormous head broke through the wall of water, its teeth snapping so close behind me that I felt the force like a slap around the back of my head. I turned the board again, but this time the shark was wise to my tricks and turned at the same time. *Oh, help! What was I going to do?*

The Megashark lunged once more, its jaw closing on the back of my board, shattering it into a thousand pieces. I plunged into the sea and found myself being swept between an outcrop of large jagged rocks, the shark hot on my heels. Once more its mouth opened . . . and then *oof!* Intent on catching me, the shark hadn't been looking where it was going, and with a revolting ripping noise that I could hear even above the roar of the wave, the predator was impaled on one of the deadly spears of rock.

With an enormous rush of relief, I curled myself up into a ball and let the water carry me through the field of granite teeth, praying that I too wouldn't end up skewered on a rock like a kebab. Then I felt the burn of gravel below me as the sea grew shallower and I was flipped and battered and tossed around like a pair of pants in a tumble dryer. And then everything went black.

Back In Bed

The kind lady who found me, battered and bruised, on the shore and carried me home and nursed me was called Ma Baldwin.

'How long have I been in bed?' I asked her.

'A week,' said Ma. 'I thought you were a goner you were so badly bruised. But a nice warm bed and old Ma Baldwin's homemade poultices did the trick, and here you are, as good as new. I don't know why you're that funny pink colour, though,' she added. 'I can't seem to give you back a nice muddy complexion.'

'I'm supposed to be this colour,' I said. 'I don't come from around here; I come from up there,' and I pointed up to the ceiling.

'Up there? Where up there?' said Ma Baldwin.

'Way up there, on the surface of the rocks.'

'You mean people live above the rock?' she exclaimed. 'I don't believe it. That's just an old wives' tale!'

'It's true, Ma,' said a voice from the shadows, making me start. 'And what's more, there's another one of 'em about.'

'Oh, Tom, you made me jump,' said Ma.

'Come and say hello to Charlie Small. This is my son, Tom, Charlie.'

Out of the gloom stepped a skinny boy about my own age (eight, that is, not four hundred!), and if I thought his ma was a muddy colour, Tom looked as if he was *made* of mud! He was a dirty browny-grey from head to foot: his hair, face, arms and clothes were caked in a thick layer of muck.

'So, you've decided to wake up at last, 'ave you?' said Tom with a grin. I liked him straight away.

'Tom's just got back from the mudflats,' said Ma. 'Now, wash your hands and come and have your tea, Tom. You can chat to Charlie while you eat.'

Exciting News

Tom ran his hands under the kitchen tap, sending streams of mud gurgling down the plughole and exposing his shiny grey skin underneath. He sat down at a rough wooden table; his mum gave him a plate of bread and a strange, dirty-white stodgy pudding, which the boy tucked into with relish.

'What have you been doing on the mudflats, Tom?' I asked. 'It looks as if you've had a lot of fun!'

'There's no fun to be 'ad down there, Charlie,' he said. 'I'm a mudskipper, a scavenger.'

'What does one of them do when it's at home?' I asked.

'I search the mudflats down by the quay, looking for scraps of food that've dropped into the drains and washed down to the shore,'

Tom's stodgy / dodgy pudding.

explained Tom, poking his fork into the sodden meal on his plate.

'You mean you found that in the mud?' I exclaimed. 'And you're eating it?'

'So what?' said Tom. 'All us kids scavenge. It's the only way we can survive.'

'Don't you ever get the runs?'

'Not if you boil everything to oblivion and back,' interrupted Ma.

'Why do you have to scavenge?' I asked, shocked at the idea of this friendly boy and his mum having to survive on scraps.

'Why? Oh, that's another story,' said Tom. 'Another story for another day, per'aps.'

I decided to change the subject.

'So, what did you mean when you said there's another person like me down here?' I asked, hoping for some news of Jakeman. Or perhaps it was one of my pirate pals from the abandoned *Betty Mae*.

'My mate Eliza said she saw a stranger with pink skin being taken to the castle a couple of weeks ago,' said Tom.

'A castle!' I cried, getting excited. 'What happens at this castle?'

'That's where the King lives, o' course,'

replied the boy.

'Huh! Some king!' Ma mumbled to herself.

'Do you know who this pink stranger is, or what he's doing there?' I asked.

'Why d'you want to know?' said Tom, suspicious all of a sudden.

'I'm looking for a friend of mine. He's the only one who can help me get home.'

Tom looked at me intensely for a moment, and then said, 'Look, Charlie, there's stuff going on down 'ere, bad stuff, and it's 'ard to know who to trust. Maybe I'll be able to 'elp when I know you better. Anyway, you look as if you need some kip. We'll have a proper chat when you're feelin' up to it.'

Oh blow! I lay back on my pillow, banging my fists on the bed and sighing in frustration. Tom was right, though; I was starting to feel tired again, and very woozy indeed.

'Don't be hard on the lad,' I heard Ma say as I drifted off to sleep. 'He don't know what's been going on . . .'

I felt very woozy!

Getting Better

I continued to feel woozy for the next couple
of days, but I've been really well looked after by
Tom and Ma.

Their house is amazing. It's carved out of
solid rock, and is warm and comfy. It's only one
room wide and three rooms high; Tom sleeps
on the top floor, Ma on the middle floor, and
my bed is made up in the kitchen on the ground
floor, where a fire blazes all day long. My bed is
surrounded by shelves laden with pots, pans and
cooking utensils, and although it's light outside,
day and night, Ma has lamps burning all the
time, and their warm golden glow makes the
house feel very cosy.

Oops! Sorry.
This is where some
Spidion spit got
onto my journal!

The worst thing, apart from being stuck in bed with my bruises, is the food – it's yuck! Ma is very apologetic, but it's not her fault; she can only cook what Tom scavenges on the mudflats, and they find the meagre scraps as hard to swallow as I do. The hairy rat sandwich I'd had was a feast compared to the poor soggy mush these Subterraneans have to survive on!

At least I've had time to bring my journal up to date, and to look through my pack of wild animal collectors cards; lo and behold, I found a card describing the mean and monstrous Megashark. This is what it says:

PREDATOR RATING 34

THE MEGASHARK

Is this leftover from the age of the dinosaur extinct? You'd better hope so! The Megashark is vicious, extremely fast and as big as a Greyhound bus. Their barbed teeth are as large as gravestones, and a gravestone is what you will probably need if you ever see one of these ferocious fish. They are scary! Chance of escape: No one has escaped so far.

WILD ANIMAL COLLECTORS CARDS

(handwritten, left margin) Yuk. This is worse than school dinners!

(handwritten, lower right) Oh yes they have!

And I couldn't agree more!

I also tried to phone home, but we're so far below ground, darn it, I couldn't get a signal! Even though my mum seems to be stuck in a time warp, and never listens to a word I say, it's good to hear the sound of her voice.

I'll have to try again when I escape from this Underworld – whenever that might be!

Getting To Know Tom

Over the next week or so, I became great friends with Tom and Ma. Every evening, after returning from the mudflats, Tom would sit at the end of my bed, chatting and joking. He was really funny and kept my spirits up as I gradually recovered from the battering I'd received; but he didn't say any more about the castle or what 'bad stuff' had been going on in Subterranea.

I talked the hind legs off a donkey, though! I told them all about how I had dropped into the Underworld, about my battles with the Spidion and the Megashark and my flight from the Troglodytes. They listened wide-eyed to my crazy adventures.

↑ The hind legs of a donkey!

'I don't know why the Trogs chased you,' said Tom. 'Most of 'em are quite friendly; my friend Eliza is good pals with some of 'em. She goes to –' But then he stopped, perhaps feeling he had said too much. I think Tom was still sizing me up, trying to work out if I could be trusted.

I didn't mind; I liked Tom, and I knew something pretty bad must have happened to make him so suspicious. He needed to feel I was a good friend before he could tell me about the 'bad stuff'. But what sort of bad stuff did he mean?

Are the Trogs friends or foe?

Blooming heck! It didn't take long for me to find out!

Tom's Close Call

One evening, as I was sitting by a roaring fire, Ma started to get very edgy. Tom was later than usual, and every few minutes she would look nervously out of the kitchen window.

'Don't worry, Ma,' I said. 'Tom will be all right.'

'You don't understand, dear,' she replied. 'He

should have been home by now.'

Just then, there was a slight clatter in the yard, the back door opened and Tom slipped in, looking pale and shaken.

'What's happened, Tom?' asked Ma anxiously. 'And where's your coat?'

'Phewee! It was a close one,' said Tom. 'I was nearly nabbed by a scruffer!'

'What on earth's a scruffer?' I asked.

'You know,' said Tom, still panting, 'a rozzer; a nabber; a so-called guardian of the law who grabs you by the scruff of the neck and shakes you till you rattle like a bag of bones.'

'A policeman?'

'You can call 'em what you like, but you don't want to get nabbed by one; especially down on the flats, or after curfew.'

'Sit down and I'll make you a nice cuppa while you tell us exactly what happened,' said Ma.

But Tom couldn't sit down. He was far too agitated.

'I was on my way 'ome from the mudflats,' he

said, his eyes bright with fear and excitement.
'I'd lost all track o' time and didn't realize it was
already past nine o'clock. No one's allowed out
after nine at night,' he explained to me. 'Anyway,
I was sneakin' through the alleys when a hand
shot out of the shadows and grabbed me by the
collar – it was a scruffer!

'"Gotcha, yer little devil," sez he, and 'e lifted
me off the ground an' spun me round to take a
closer look at me face. "Why, you filfy little so
an' so! You been down on them mudflats, ain't
ya?" he said.

'"So what if I 'ave?" I cried, and gave 'im a
mighty kick on the shin! Oh, you should've 'eard
'im yell! But 'e didn't let go.

'"Let's 'ave
a proper look
at yer," 'e said,
'oppin' about
on one leg. 'E
was just about
to wipe my
face clean with
'is 'anky when
I slipped out
of me coat,

dropped to the ground and legged it back 'ere!

'"Come back, you varmint," 'e yelled. "I'll 'ave yer guts for garters!"'

'He didn't follow you, did he?' asked Ma nervously. She passed Tom a cup of hot, muddy tea and a rock cake – made out of real powdered rock!

Mmm! One of Ma's <u>rock</u> cakes!

'No chance,' said Tom confidently.

Just then, there was a loud banging on the front door!

'Scruffers!' said Ma. 'Tom – the hideaway, quick!'

A Right Ruckus In The House

'Just coming!' called Ma as Tom hurriedly pulled back the kitchen rug. To my amazement, he put his fingers through a small crack in the floorboards and lifted a hidden hatchway.

A flight of steps led down into darkness.

'Hurry up, Tom,' said Ma – the knocking was growing louder. 'You too, Charlie; he mustn't find *you* here.'

I followed Tom down the steps. Ma closed the hatch behind us and threw the carpet back into place. We heard her footsteps as she hurried to the front door; we heard her drawing back the bolts, and the crash of the door as it was kicked open.

Then came the sound of heavy footsteps, marching into the kitchen. I found a small gap at the edge of the rug and looked up through the narrow gaps between the boards. I saw a scruffer for the very first time; what a scary sight he was!

I could see why Ma and Tom were so afraid of him. From his high plumed hat to his gleaming black boots, his uniform said just one thing: bully!

'Where is 'e?' demanded the scruffer.

'Where's who?' asked Ma innocently.

'I saw a boy run in 'ere. A boy off the mudflats, out after curfew.'

'I don't know what you mean, I'm sure,' said Ma.

The
Scruffer

'Then you won't mind me 'aving a look round, will ya?'

'Be my guest, but you won't find anything,' said Ma.

The Scruffer Searches For Tom

The scruffer stormed around the kitchen, flinging open cupboards and emptying their contents onto the floor.

'If I find 'im, it'll be straight to the mines with 'im for a spot of 'ard labour,' growled the obnoxious oaf. He searched the pantry, pulling empty cartons and boxes off the shelves, muttering and swearing to himself all the time. His heavy boots scraped and clumped on the floorboards, just inches above our heads.

'Keep quiet,' Tom whispered to me, 'or we'll be in dead trouble.'

I didn't need telling twice. What would happen if

CRUNCH!

we were hauled away by this cretinous creature didn't bear thinking about.

Not finding anything in the kitchen, the scruffer stormed upstairs, and again we heard banging and crashing as he searched the bedrooms.

'Who sleeps in the top room?' he asked, stomping back downstairs.

'My son,' Ma told him.

'And why ain't 'e at 'ome right now? You know it's against the law to be out after nine o'clock.'

'He's staying with a friend,' said Ma. 'That's not against the law as well now, is it?'

The scruffer growled, 'I'm sure I saw 'im come in 'ere.'

'Well, you were wrong, weren't you,' replied Ma. 'Now if you've quite finished, I'd like to get to bed.'

'Who sleeps there?' demanded the man, pointing at my tangle of sheets on the sofa.

'Oh, er, I've been sleeping there,' said Ma, thinking quickly. 'I've had a chill and spent a few nights in front of the fire. Satisfied?'

'Not really,' he said, marching to the door. 'I 'aven't been able to find anythin', but I know

I'll be keeping an eye on you!

you've been up to somethin'. I'll be keepin' an eye on you, missus, so be warned.' And with that, he marched out into the street, slamming the door behind him.

'All clear,' said Ma after a few minutes. She pulled up the hatch and Tom and I climbed back into the kitchen.

'Phewee! What fun,' said Tom, and burst out laughing. 'Well done, Charlie. I knew I could trust you! Tomorrow I'll bring a friend of mine to meet you. We can tell you everythin' that's been going on in Subterranea and see if we can come up with a plan to find your friend.'

Brilliant! That's more like it; maybe it won't be too long before I find Jakeman and continue my journey.

Eliza

Tom was as good as his word, and the next day he arrived home with a girl by his side. She was about seven years old, short and slight, and dressed in muddy rags.

She was obviously a mudskipper too, and in her hand she carried a collecting bag for her finds on the mudflats.

It oozed a thick dribble of sludge that dripped down her ragged dress. She had the same grey skin and large, round head that all the Subterraneans seem to have, with a small,

Eliza

determined mouth and big bright eyes.

'This is Charlie Small, who I've been tellin' you about,' said Tom. 'Charlie, this is my best pal and fellow mudskipper, Eliza.'

'Pleased to meet you, Eliza,' I said.

'Likewise, I'm sure,' said Eliza, staring curiously at my pink face.

'She's the one who saw the stranger bein' taken to the castle,' explained Tom.

My heart leaped. 'Did you manage to get a good look at him?' I asked.

'All I can tell you is that 'e was a small, pink, whiskery old man,' said the muddy girl. 'Some scruffers took 'im there, but I don't know what 'appened to 'im after that.'

'That's got to be Jakeman,' I cried. 'But how on earth am I going to find him if the scruffers have got him?'

'Well, I might be able to 'elp you there. I know a secret way into the castle,' said Tom.

'You do?' I cried. 'Well, what are we waiting for? Let's go!'

''Old your 'orses,' said Tom. 'First you need to know what's been going on in Subterranea and what we're up against.'

'The bad stuff that's happened?'

'The bad stuff,' said Tom, pulling up a chair for Eliza and sitting cross-legged on the floor in front of the fire.

This was it! At last I was going to find out *exactly* what was going on in Subterranea. And Tom was right – it was really bad . . .

The Bad Stuff

As Ma busied herself at the kitchen range, sorting and preparing Tom's finds for our dinner, my two muddy friends explained how life in Subterranea had changed for the worse.

'It all started when the King got 'imself a new adviser,' said Tom. 'Before that 'e was really nice and everyone was 'appy. I went to school with all me mates, and Ma curled feathers to go on posh 'ats. And food? Oh, we 'ad loads of food. Every week, carts piled high with vegetables from the allotments would line up in the square. Things were great.'

A curly feather!

'Then, one day, this new chap arrived on the scene,' said Eliza. 'We don't know where 'e came from, but 'e's really creepy. 'E wears a long black coat and a wide black hat and covers 'is face with a spooky metal mask. All we know about 'im is that 'e's secretive and scary, and 'e's got some sort of 'old over our poor King. Everyone calls him the Shadow. 'E's absolutely vile!'

Ooo-err! I didn't like the sound of this, and a cold shudder went zigzagging down my spine.

The Shadow

'Some people think 'e wears a mask because 'e's really an 'orrible robot,' said Tom. 'We reckon it's because 'e's an outsider and 'e's trying to 'ide 'is pink skin. That's why I was a bit suspicious of you at first; I thought you might 'ave somethin' to do with 'im.'

'Oh, thanks a million!' I said. 'Do I look like the side-kick of a vile, flesh-crawling creep?'

'Na, you're OK,' said Tom, grinning. Then he became very serious again. 'I don't think you realize just what a downright bad-'un the

Shadow is. As soon as 'e turned up, the King started passin' really strict laws, and everythin' in Subterranea turned bad.'

The Scruffers enforce the law with an iron fist!

'Really bad,' said Eliza. 'The very first thing 'e did was set up the scruffers, to keep us all in order. You know how nasty they can be.'

'Then 'e formed the Trog Guard, an army of the most vicious Troglodytes 'e could find,' continued Tom. ''E ordered 'em to invade Barbaria, their very own country, and capture all the remainin' Trogs and turn 'em into slaves!'

Pooeee!

'Big pig!' said Eliza.

'Really, Eliza! Language please,' said Ma, stirring something smelly in a large pot on the stove.

'Well, 'e bloomin' well is,' said Eliza. ''E makes the

poor Trog slaves dig and dig all day long, minin'
the precious light from our cavern rock – but
what for? It all seems so pointless!'

'Now, all the food from our allotments goes
to feed the Shadow's henchmen,' said Tom.
'The tiny bit that's left over is given to the slaves.
That's why we 'ave to scavenge for our food.'

'That's terrible! Why don't the people of
Subterranea do something about it?' I asked
naively. 'Surely the King would listen if he's as
nice as you say.'

'We've tried, of course we have,' said Ma,
getting upset and banging our knives and forks
down on the table. 'Some of the men went
to the gates and demanded to be let in. They
disappeared inside the castle . . . and that's the
last we ever saw of them!'

'And these are the people that've got hold of
your friend Jakeman,' said Eliza.

'Jeepers creepers! Poor old Jakeman; and poor
old you! We've got to do something,' I cried.

'Yes, well, you can worry about that after
dinner,' said Ma. 'Who's for some Scrappy
Stew?'

Oh, blimey! I thought. What delicious
delights go into Scrappy Stew?

A Funny Find In My Dinner!

Ma ladled some stew into our bowls. We knew it was made of Tom's muddy finds, but we were really hungry and tucked in. It was nice – well, as nice as it could be!

There were some bits of greenish meat (not more rat, I hope!) and I'm sure there was a grape or two floating in the gritty gravy. There were pieces of carrot and half a jam tart; an elastic band (that was quite nice) and something that looked just like a pig's nose; but it was Eliza who discovered the most surprising ingredient.

'What's this?' she asked, lifting her spoon out of the bowl. Hanging there, steaming and dripping with sauce, was a pair of spectacles!

'Well, they're not mine,' said Ma.

'I must've picked 'em up on the flats,' said Tom.

'Let's have a look,' I said, and Eliza passed them over. 'Hey, these are Jakeman's specs!'

'That *proves* 'e's in the castle,' said Tom. 'That's where the drains come from.'

'So how are we going to find him?' I said.

'I've got an idea . . .' said Tom.

Tom's Story

'I've been secretly visitin' the castle, tryin' to find out what's goin' on up there,' continued Tom, talking with his mouth full. 'There's a quay nearby. It sticks out over the mudflats, on big wooden pillars. Right at the back where the mudflats meet the 'arbour wall are the openin's to the big drains.

'One day, when I was feelin' brave, I decided to crawl up one of the drainpipes to see where it went. I came to a big metal grille, which I managed to loosen and crawl through. I found myself in a secret passage *inside* the castle walls!'

'That's incredible!' I exclaimed.

'It's flippin' fantastic,' said Tom. 'Lots of the walls have secret passages, and they go all over the castle. Look, I've drawn a plan so I don't get lost.' He pulled a filthy piece of paper from his pocket and showed it to me. This is just a bit of it (Tom gave me this as a souvenir; the rest got torn off):

1st floor
Guards

Door

throne room
1st floor ✗

Peep hole

Stairs in secret passage

Ground floor
Dining room

Secret passages in the wall

↑ Main Staircase

Waiter's room

up
Grille in floor

Great Hall

Kitchen
Ground floor

Square

← Castle Keep

Door.
Courtyard.

Secret passages

Castle's Outer Wall

↗ route

Main Gate

Tower

Square

Not to scale.

← Main drain

Mudflats

in

Jetty

Sea

Secret Passages

The walls inside the castle are hollow, making passages that skirt all round the rooms.

'What do you do about going up and down stairs?' I asked.

'That's the most amazin' thing,' said Tom. 'If a corridor goes up some steps, the secret passage has steps too. You can wander up and down between all the floors. Well, most of the time, anyway. Sometimes you 'ave to climb out of an air vent and sneak along the castle corridors. But there's always another grille that gets you back into the secret passage.'

'What's this big X for?' I asked.

'That's the King's throne room,' said Tom.

'Wow! Have you ever seen him?'

'I've seen 'im,' said Tom, 'but I didn't dare talk to 'im – there was a huge Trog guard outside the door.'

'What I'd like to know is, what's happened to the Queen?' said Ma suddenly. 'No one's seen her for ages.'

'There's no sign of 'er in the castle,' said Tom.

'Oh, dearie me! What is going on up there?'

cried Ma, getting agitated again. 'What are we going to do?'

'Don't worry, Ma, we'll think of something,' said Tom. 'Won't we, Lize?'

Eliza's Story

'What we need is a mutiny!' said Eliza, chewing extra hard on a piece of gristle. 'I've been meetin' with the Trog slaves in secret. They sleep in a big hollow in the ground, all shackled together. Some nights, I creep past the guards and clamber down into the Trogs' crater. I've been tryin' to persuade 'em to stand up to the Shadow's cronies, and *fight*.'

'You must be crackers, creeping about in craters after curfew!' said Ma.

'How do you speak to the Trogs?' I asked. 'They only seem to know one word – *Man-cha*!'

'I've been tryin' to teach 'em English, but they 'ave trouble sayin' the words. So I made up a really simple sign language. Now we understand each other fine,' said Eliza. 'They're really clever, and they're kind too.'

'Really?' I said, thinking once again that I had

misjudged these poor creatures. 'Are they willing to fight?'

'They're not ready yet. They're scared to death of the Shadow,' said Eliza. 'If they just look at 'im funny, 'e 'as them thrown into the fiery pit to fry.'

'Jumping Jehoshaphat!' I cried. That's what those bones were in the Spidion's web.

'They might fight if they 'ad some 'elp,' said Eliza.

'What if the townspeople were to join them?' asked Ma. 'I'm sure they'd love to help defeat the Shadow and his guards – especially if it means we'll get our lovely King and Queen back.'

'D'you think they would?' asked Eliza. 'I reckon that might make all the difference.'

'We need a plan!' I said, banging the table and making the salt and pepper pots jump. 'A plan to crush the sinister Shadow and all his cronies!'

'You bet,' said Tom. 'And this is what I think we should do –'

All of a sudden there was a terrible clatter

amongst the dustbins in the back yard. Tom leaped up.

'Someone's been listenin',' he said, and peered out of the window.

'Who's there?' asked Ma, getting up herself and fiddling nervously with her apron. 'Not a stupid scruffer, I hope.'

'Phew!' said Tom, turning round and giving us one of his widest grins. 'Panic over! It was only a daft rockfox at the bins.'

(Later on, Tom described a rockfox to me. I did this drawing, and he said it was pretty good!)

A Rockfox!

A Plan And A Pact

Ma drew the curtains and we all sat down again, huddling together around the table.

'Here's the plan,' said Tom. 'Charlie and I will go to the castle first thing tomorrow. We need to find out who the Shadow is and what sort of power 'e 'as over the King. Then we must find out what's 'appened to the Queen and we need to locate your pal.'

'If it is Jakeman in the castle, I'm sure he'll lend a hand,' I said. 'He's a brilliant inventor and might be able to come up with some sort of gadget to help us.'

'And then we might 'ave ourselves a mutiny!'

'I'll pass the word round the neighbourhood that the time to make a stand is getting near,' said Ma.

'And I'm goin' to sneak back to see the slave Trogs tonight and tell 'em to be prepared,' said Eliza. 'This is excitin'; somethin' big might be about to 'appen!'

'Agreed?' asked Tom.

'Agreed!' we replied. Then we spat on our hands and clasped them together to seal our pact. Even good old Ma!

Now I'm lying in bed, trying to get some sleep before our big day tomorrow. It's not easy: I'm only just starting to realize what I've agreed to! I'm going to creep inside a castle, where a mysterious, shadowy enemy holds sway over the whole of the Underworld. I'm going to try and help start a revolution! Goodness knows what will happen if the Shadow gets hold of us . . .

A Cunning Disguise!

Next morning, after a breakfast of bread crusts and fried bacon rind, Tom took me out to their little back yard. It stood in a pool of light from the glowing rock sky, and was hemmed in by the great grey walls of the surrounding houses.

Ma kept the yard spotlessly clean, and stacked on all sides were wooden tubs filled with a mass of colourful flowers. Tom reached into one of the containers and pulled out a handful of rich, smelly soil.

'Spread this over your face,' he said.

'You must be joking,' I replied. 'Why would I want to do that?'

'To hide your skin, o' course. All Subterraneans 'ave grey skin. You'll stand out like a sore thumb with your pink face, and if a scruffer sees you, you'll be in real trouble.'

'Ah! If you put it like that . . .' I said, kneeling down. I collected handfuls of mud and covered my face and hands. I rubbed it into my hair until it was as dark as Tom's, and soon you couldn't tell us apart.

I was covered in mud from head to foot!

'Perfect,' said Tom with a grin. 'Let's get goin'.'

Down On The Flats

Poor old Ma looked very worried when we said cheerio.

'Oh, do be careful, boys,' she said, wringing the tea towel in her hands. 'I hate the thought of you sneaking into that dangerous place. It's like creeping into a lion's den! Don't do anything silly, and don't be late for tea.'

'Don't worry, we'll be all right,' said Tom confidently. 'I been there before. What could possibly go wrong?'

I followed Tom out into the narrow alleyway that ran between the houses. If I'd had my wits about me, I should have guessed something *would* go wrong, because that's almost exactly what Mum said to me, about four hundred years ago, when I first left to go out on my raft.

Turning left and right, I followed Tom down one lane after another, past rows of houses and tiny, open-fronted stores. The lanes were thronged with people, but the food stores were empty, and I understood why Tom had resorted to scavenging on the mudflats.

The winding streets of Subterranea were like one of those mazes you get in activity books; the kind where you have to find the route that leads to some treasure or something, and I knew that if I lost sight of Tom for an instant, I would never find my way back to his house again.

All the buildings had been carved from the blue-grey rock of the great cavern; their

Tom's house

Scruffer.

It was like a maze castle.
in an activity book!

walls were rough with the marks of a mason's chisel and in patches, where veins of the phosphorescent mineral were embedded, they glowed, lighting up the alleyways.

Eventually, when I was totally confused and had lost all sense of direction, Tom stopped me and peered round a corner.

'We really don't want a scruffer to spot us,' he said, looking left and right. 'Now! Come on!' And he was off again. I followed, hot on his heels, out of the narrow alley and into a wide, open square, where I saw the castle for the first time!

The Castle

The great fortress loomed high above us, and I stopped and stared in wonder. Its thick walls had been painted white, making the whole palace shine under the rock light. The conical roofs of its huge towers were covered with terracotta tiles and it looked just like a fairytale castle.

The Castle.

Before I had time to take it all in, Tom pulled my sleeve and we went racing across the square towards the quayside, where a series of jetties stuck out over the muddy shore of the Wide Subterrestrial Sea.

'Jump!' yelled Tom, and I launched myself from the end of the jetty and landed with a squelch, knee-deep in the mud of the flats below. 'This way,' he went on, guiding me under the jetty and towards the harbour wall, where a series of wide drainpipes led under the square.

The MudSkippers

As I got used to the gloom under the jetty, I realized we were not alone. There was a crowd of children, all up to their calves in mud, bent double and silently sifting through the gloopy gunge with their hands.

Occasionally, one of them would bring up an item from the mud, rinse it in a puddle, examine it and either throw it back or put it in a sack hanging from their belt.

'Mornin', Tom,' came a voice from the shadows, and Eliza came over, mud dripping from her collecting bag. 'You all set?'

'Sure,' said Tom. I wished I had his confidence, because my knees were knocking together like a pair of castanets! 'How did it go with the Trog slaves last night?'

'Good news! It's just like we 'oped,' said Eliza, her big eyes shining bright in the gloom. 'If the townsfolk will 'elp, the Trog slaves will fight their dreaded guards! They're just waitin' for the word.'

RAT-A-TAT-TAT!

'Brilliant,' said Tom. 'But first Charlie and I need to recce the castle. We'll know more when we've talked to the King and tracked down Charlie's friend. Let's meet at my 'ouse this evenin'. Then we can put the last touches to our plans!'

'You bet,' said Eliza. 'Good luck.'

'Ready, Charlie?' asked Tom. 'Come on then. I'll take you right to the 'eart of the castle – the King's throne room!'

I gave a loud gulp as we waded through the thick mud into the deepest shadows below the quayside.

Down The Drains!

I followed Tom into the mouth of the drain that led under the cobbled square and right beneath the castle itself. As soon as the light faded, he reached into his pocket and pulled out a lump of stone marbled with the phosphorescent mineral that illuminated the whole of the great cavern. It gave off enough light for us to find our way along the wide, stinking waterway.

We waded through ankle-deep sludge, and every now and then Tom's hand darted into the murky water and brought out a scrap of food. It was as if he had a sixth sense because I couldn't see anything at all, and soon his bag was bulging with his meagre finds. All I was aware of was the overpowering smell of rancid food and stagnant water.

After a while the tunnel widened out into a brick-lined, arched chamber, into which a number of other drainage channels emptied.

'This way,' whispered Tom, leading me along the new channel, which climbed steeply until it levelled out below an iron grille. Looking up, I could see we were under the castle's huge and busy kitchen. Above us, the Head Chef was barking orders to his team of Sous Chefs, Pastry Chefs and Line Cooks, who were frantically chopping and rolling and salting the food that filled the tables.

The head chef.

'Oh, just smell that delicious food!' said Tom, closing his eyes and holding his rumbling tummy. 'And to think it must be going to feed the Shadow and his henchmen, while my poor old ma is sitting at 'ome with only a crust of bread. It ain't fair.'

Just then, a scrap of raw pastry dropped off one of the tables and fell right through the grille. Tom's hand shot out as fast as a striking snake, caught it and put it in his sack.

'Come on,' he whispered, pulling on my sleeve, and we carried on along the drain below the kitchen, past a series of small and extremely smelly pipes, until we were standing below another grille. This time Tom signalled for a leg-up and I clasped my hands together into a stirrup for his foot.

I hoisted him up and Tom pushed at the iron grating. It fell back with a clatter, and he waited for the noise to die away before levering himself through the hole. As soon as he was up, he pulled me after him.

Between the Walls

Now we were in a tall, dry passage. I followed Tom as he crept along, holding up his piece of light rock and glancing every now and then at his plan of the castle. Soon we came to where a new passage led off to the left.

'This way,' whispered Tom. Just then, I tripped over some loose stones and fell against the side wall.

'Shhh! A Trog guard might hear us!'

'Sorry!' I whispered, and followed more carefully.

We took another turn, and climbed some little stone steps to the next floor. Soon I could see a square of light ahead, and as we got nearer I saw it was a ventilation grille set into the wall.

'Take a look,' whispered Tom, and I peered over his shoulder. There, sitting on his throne and staring into space, was the King, a tiny, mud-grey little man, and possibly the saddest-looking person I've ever seen.

The King Of Subterranea

The King sat with his head in his hands, sighing and muttering to himself.

'I won't have it,' he said. 'Enough is enough. I've got to tell him straight: I'm in charge and he's got to clear off and leave my people alone. Yes, that's what I'll do. He doesn't scare me . . . Oh dear, who am I trying to kid? What on earth can I do?'

Just then, the big doors to the throne room burst open with a crash, and in stormed a tall man dressed in black.

The Shadow Of Subterranea In Person!

A shudder went down my spine as the malevolent masked figure marched up to the King. His hat was pulled down low on his head, which was thrust forward from his long black coat like a tortoise peering from its shell. The scariest thing about him was the shiny metal mask that covered his face. It was sharp and angular, with a spike of a nose and a long, vicious-looking chin. The figure's piercing, angry eyes blazed from behind two narrow slits.

'That's the Shadow,' whispered Tom a little unnecessarily.

'I guessed that!' I said.

'You wanted to see me,' the Shadow said impatiently. 'What do you want? Hurry up, I haven't got all day.'

The King stood up nervously. 'I – I've had enough!' he stammered. 'You've got to stop treating my subjects so badly – you've –'

'WHAT?' bellowed the Shadow, shaking with anger.

'Give my people food,' said the King, his voice fading away to a petrified squeak. 'They are starving. I want you out of here, you great bully.'

'Good for you, Your Majesty,' whispered Tom. 'Stand up to the creep.'

'Aren't you forgetting who's in charge here?' growled the Shadow, stepping threateningly towards the King. 'Aren't you forgetting about your pretty, precious wife?'

The King collapsed back onto the throne. 'What have you done with her?' he asked. 'When can I see her again?'

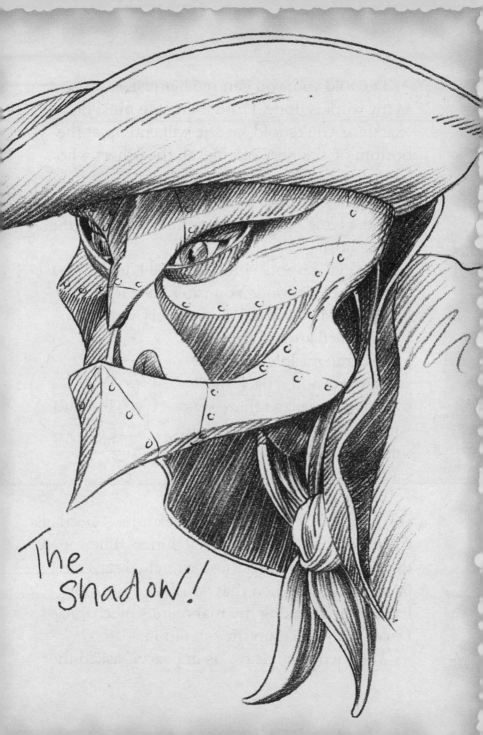

The
shadow!

'I've told you: you can see her just as soon as my work is done. Until then, you must do exactly as you're told, or she will end up at the bottom of the fiery pit, like all the others who have dared to disobey me.'

'So that's why the Shadow 'as such power over the King,' whispered Tom. 'He's taken the Queen hostage.'

'You evil despot!' screeched the King. 'At least give my people food. You can't need it all.'

The Shadow started to get angry again. He marched around the room, gesticulating wildly; and somewhere at the back of my mind, I realized there was something very familiar about this figure. *You know this man*, I said to myself. *But who is he?*

'When are you going to learn, you royal twit,' thundered the Shadow. 'I need all the food I can get for my henchmen. They need their strength to keep these wretched slaves in order. Soon, when that whiskered buffoon has finished making my marvellous mechanical mole, I can speed up my operation.'

'And then you'll leave us in peace?' asked the

miserable King.

'And then I'll leave you in peace . . . and in darkness, I'm afraid, for I intend to take every last seam of light that runs through this godforsaken Underworld.'

'But if you leave us in the dark, there's no way my people will survive!'

'Not my problem, Your Majesty. All I'm interested in is taking the rocks of light above ground. Imagine the riches I will accrue, selling this miraculous mineral up there. No more need for oil lamps, or gas lamps, or electric light bulbs. Whole cities are going to be illuminated by my rock light, and I will be the richest man in the world before a month has passed. Ha-ha, ha-ha!'

'You're nothing but a cowardy custard, hiding behind that mask,' said the King. 'If I knew the Queen was safe, I would kick you out of my kingdom for good.'

'Oh, you are so amusing, Your Majesty,' laughed the Shadow. 'Now, if that's all you wanted, I must go and see how the idiot inventor is getting on with my mole!' With that he turned

A cowardy custard!

on his heel and swept out of the throne room.

'Come on,' I said. 'We've got to follow him. He said he's going to see the inventor. That must be Jakeman. *He*'ll know what to do.'

'OK!' said Tom. 'Let's go!'

Sneaking About Like Rats!

We rushed along the secret passage and down some steps to another air vent in the wall. Looking out, we saw the Shadow crossing the great hall.

'What now?' I asked, watching our quarry disappear through a small door on the far side.

'Don't worry,' said Tom. 'I've been through 'ere before.' He gave the grating a good tug,

There's a lot of dirty rats in this castle!

pulling it from the wall with hardly a sound, and we stepped cautiously into the hall.

'Quiet now!' he hissed, replacing the grating into the hole. 'The throne room is just at the top of that big flight of stairs. We must make sure the guards don't see us.'

We scampered noiselessly across the great hall, crouching low and dodging behind bits of furniture to avoid being seen.

Then we were through the door on the far side and pattering down a narrow spiral staircase, until we were deep beneath the castle; deeper even than the drains we had entered by. We came to a long, dark passage. It was lined with wide buttresses to support the rickety walls, and there, right at the other end, was the Shadow. He was standing with his back towards us, outside a heavy door with a barred window in the middle.

'Quick!' I whispered, and we dived behind a buttress for cover. I watched as the Shadow took a key from his pocket and unlocked the door. Then he did the most surprising thing. He reached under his chin and ripped away the mask . . . *and I got the shock of my life!*

An Old, Old Enemy!

← Help! Boo Hiss!

'It's Craik!' I croaked before I could stop myself.

I'd recognize that face anywhere, with its large, square jaw and the livid scar running through the stubble of the left cheek.

CRAIK! HELP!

Craik spun round to see where the noise had come from. He clumped along the passage in his heavy shoes, looking about him. Finally, he stopped, just the other side of our hiding place. Everything went very quiet, and Tom and I held our breath, our hearts beating like billy-o! Eventually, Craik turned and marched back along the passage. He heaved open the door and went inside. Tom and I let out our breath.

'Close one!' whispered Tom. 'Who's Craik?'

'He's a double-crossing, low-down, no-good son of a snake,' I replied.

'Wow! You really don't like 'im, do you?' said Tom.

'He's my deadliest enemy, Tom. I robbed him when I sailed with the pirates and he swore to follow me to the ends of the earth and see me hang!'

Just then, we heard raised voices coming from the room ahead.

'That's Jakeman!' I said. 'Stay here, Tom. I'm going to have a closer look.'

'No, Charlie . . .' whispered Tom, but I was already halfway to the door. It was standing ajar, and I warily peered round it.

There, in a room brightly lit by rock lights,

was my friend Jakeman. At last I'd found him! He stood next to a huge machine that had a tangled mass of wires spewing from its side.

It was a huge grey hulk of a thing, made of thick metal plates and bolted together with a thousand rivets. At one end of the contraption was a large corkscrew nose, encircled by a spiral blade edged with glittering diamonds. It was awesome.

Around it hung tools of every description; workbenches and lathes stood along one side of the room; plans and working drawings littered the floor, and Jakeman's scribbles covered a large blackboard against the far wall.

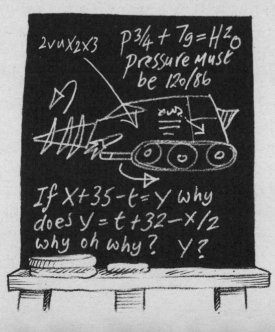

Hurrah! I've found Jakeman.

'I can't say when it will be ready,' Jakeman was explaining. 'A week, maybe two.'

'That's not good enough, you old fool,' screamed Craik. Then, stepping towards my pal, he grabbed him round the throat. 'I've a good mind to fling you into the pit,' he growled.

I gasped in fear, and this time Craik not only heard me – but with one swift movement he dropped Jakeman, swept over to the door and grabbed me by the scruff of the neck as I tried to scramble away. With a loud hiss, like the low-down snake he was, Craik threw me into the room.

Jakeman At Last!

I landed next to the huge, oily machine.

'Charlie!' cried Jakeman, helping me to my feet.

'Hello, Mr Jakeman.' I smiled. 'I've been looking for you!'

'Well, well, if it isn't my old pal, Charlie Small,' spat Craik, curling his top lip into a sneer and exposing a row of rotting teeth. 'I thought you might turn up, you little pest.'

'I thought *you'd* been squished under the Icicle Arch,' I said defiantly.

(See my Journal The Puppet Master)

'Oh, *you wish!*' said Craik. 'I'll tell you exactly what happened, shall I, you interfering worm? When you sent that colossal load of ice crashing down on top of me, the ground started to rumble and shudder beneath my feet. It split wide open, and I dropped right in. I fell and fell for such a long time I thought I would fall right through the earth! But, luckily for me, I ended up in the Underworld . . . and I didn't have a scratch on me!'

'And now you've bullied your way into taking over the whole of Subterranea. Typical!' I cried.

'Yes, I've managed to make quite a go of it down here,' he said with a smirk. 'It's surprising what a creepy mask and a royal prisoner can do. Anyone who stands in my way ends up at the bottom of a big, fiery pit. It's so easy – like taking candy from a baby.'

'And what's with the silly mask? It's not scary,' I lied.

'Oh, I think it is,' said Craik, holding it up. 'Without it I'd be just a pink outsider. No more scary than you, Charlie. With this I'm terrifying; horrific; EVIL!'

To be quite honest, I thought he looked scarier without it.

'But even though I've been busy down here, I never forgot my promise to you, Charlie,' said Craik. 'I have spies everywhere, and I heard all about your pathetic victories with the Daredevil Desperados of Destiny, and how you met up with Jakeman.

'It just so happens I had need of Jakeman too, and when I heard he was trekking across the desert with a small boy in tow, I sent one of my Troglodyte guards up the tubes to get you both. Imagine my disappointment when he only turned up with one of my prizes; but I knew you wouldn't be able to resist your meddling. I knew you'd be along eventually.'

'Clear off, Craik,' I muttered. 'You didn't scare me then and you don't scare me now.'

'Yes, leave him alone, or you'll be sorry,' growled Jakeman.

Another Horrible Surprise! (Yikes!!)

'Big talk for a small boy and an old man,' scoffed Craik. 'Oh, I forgot – there's another friend of yours you might like to meet, Charlie; someone who's been helping me. I found her abandoned on the *Betty Mae*. Heaven knows how that old wreck ended up in the Wide Subterrestrial Sea, but she did, and who was still on board but – No, just a minute, here she is. Why don't you say hello yourself?'

I turned round, not knowing who to expect – Captain Cut-throat perhaps, or Rawcliffe Annie, or any one of the bloodthirsty pirates I had sailed with. But it was worse than that. Much worse.

'Bobo!' I squealed as the malicious mandrill padded into the room. I'd hoped never to see her again. Bobo sat

Bobo bared her teeth.

back on her haunches and bared her teeth in an ear-splitting scream.

'Charlie Small!' she grunted in Ape language, giving me a look of pure hatred. 'Oh, how utterly delicious; what terrible chores can I dream up for you?'

'I thought you'd be pleased to see your old pal. And you do remember my promise, don't you, Charlie?' said Craik, sticking out his tongue and miming someone being hanged. 'For now, though, you can stay and help this idiot inventor finish my mining machine. Get a move on – you've got two days or it will turn out bad for the boy.'

With that the pernicious pair swept out of the room and locked the door behind them.

I hate Bobo. True!

Back With Jakeman

I can't believe it – I'm a prisoner again. And as if that's not bad enough, I'm a prisoner of two of my oldest and deadliest enemies – Craik and Bobo!

At least I've found my pal Jakeman, though. It was great to see him again, and as soon as our two adversaries left, Jakeman patted me on the head and tousled my hair.

'How on earth did you manage to get here, Charlie?' he said. 'Don't tell me you've been having more of your incredible adventures, m' boy?'

'You bet,' I said, and gave him a quick summing up of all my escapades since we'd been separated in the desert.

He looked astonished. He sat down on his inventor's stool and wiped his brow with an oily handkerchief. 'Amazing!' he said. 'Utterly amazing!'

Then I told him what Craik had been up to as the sinister Shadow. I told him about Tom, Eliza and Ma, and our plan.

'Dear, oh dear, I didn't know things were so serious,' said Jakeman. 'I *had* worked out that Craik was a nasty piece of work, but I didn't know about the Trog slaves; I didn't know about the King and Queen and the poor townspeople. You're right: we *must* help them. Oh, what a fool I've been!'

Craik or the Shadow.

$$x + 7/2^3 \div 76 \times \sqrt{9} + 25 = \text{Craik is a nasty piece of work!}$$

'What do you mean?' I asked.

'When I was dragged down into the Underworld, I was brought straight to this wonderful laboratory. Craik apologized for kidnapping me, but said it was a matter of life and death for the poor people of Subterranea.

'He knew I was a famous inventor, and he asked me to build him a special machine; a machine that could do the work of a thousand miners. He said his poor Trogs were exhausted and he wanted to give them a rest. He was full of flattery, and I fell for every lie. But not any more, Charlie; I want to help too, and I reckon this machine is just what we need!'

'What good would that be?' I asked.

'Think about it, Charlie,' he said, starting to fiddle with the wires on his machine again. 'If you and your friends are going to start a battle, just imagine what this beast could do. It's as powerful as an army tank!'

'You're right!' I cried. 'It will scare the pants off the guards. Brilliant! I knew you'd come up with the answer.'

'Hold your horses,' said Jakeman. 'We've got to know that your plan is in place first. We can't fight a mutiny on our own. And I must get this

bloomin' mechanical
mole to work. Now,
is this a red wire, or a
brown one?'

'Oh!' I said, searching
through my rucksack. 'I think these might be
yours!'

'My specs!' Jakeman smiled. 'Charlie, you are
a wonder. Maybe now I can see what I'm doing
and get this machine working!'

Thinking...

While Jakeman works on his mechanical mole,
I've been writing my journal and trying to figure
things out.

Is there a way out of this laboratory so I can
help Tom and Eliza carry on with our plan?
I've had a look and there aren't any air vents
or secret passages down here. Could I use my
hunting knife to dig through the laboratory wall?
Will I end up dangling from the end of Craik's
noose, or at the bottom of a fiery pit?

'Of course, when the time comes, the mole
can also get us out of the Underworld and

back into the sunshine,'
Jakeman continued,
proudly patting the
side of his great
machine. A fountain
of sparks shot from
the end of the wires
he was holding,
sending him leaping
into the air.

This must be one of the glowing bug's feathery legs that the ape-man knocked off — ouch! Poor thing.

'Ooh! Blast — got a shock!' he
said, and I couldn't help grinning, because his
hair was standing up on end like a peacock's tail
feathers!

'How is *that* going to help us?' I chuckled.

The Mole ← Brilliant!

'The mole is a mining machine and can slice
through rock like a knife through butter,'
Jakeman told me. 'All we need to do is turn it on
and burrow our way up to the surface. Look . . .'
He unpinned one of his plans from the wall and
passed it over. This is the piece of paper he gave
me:

A Jakeman Invention
THE MOLE

Diamond edged spiral blade

Rotating nose cone

Electro-sensitive feelers

Powerful spotlights

Diamond encrusted tunnelling nose tip

Arm scoops to remove larger waste material

Brush fringed vacuum chute

Patent No. 102757

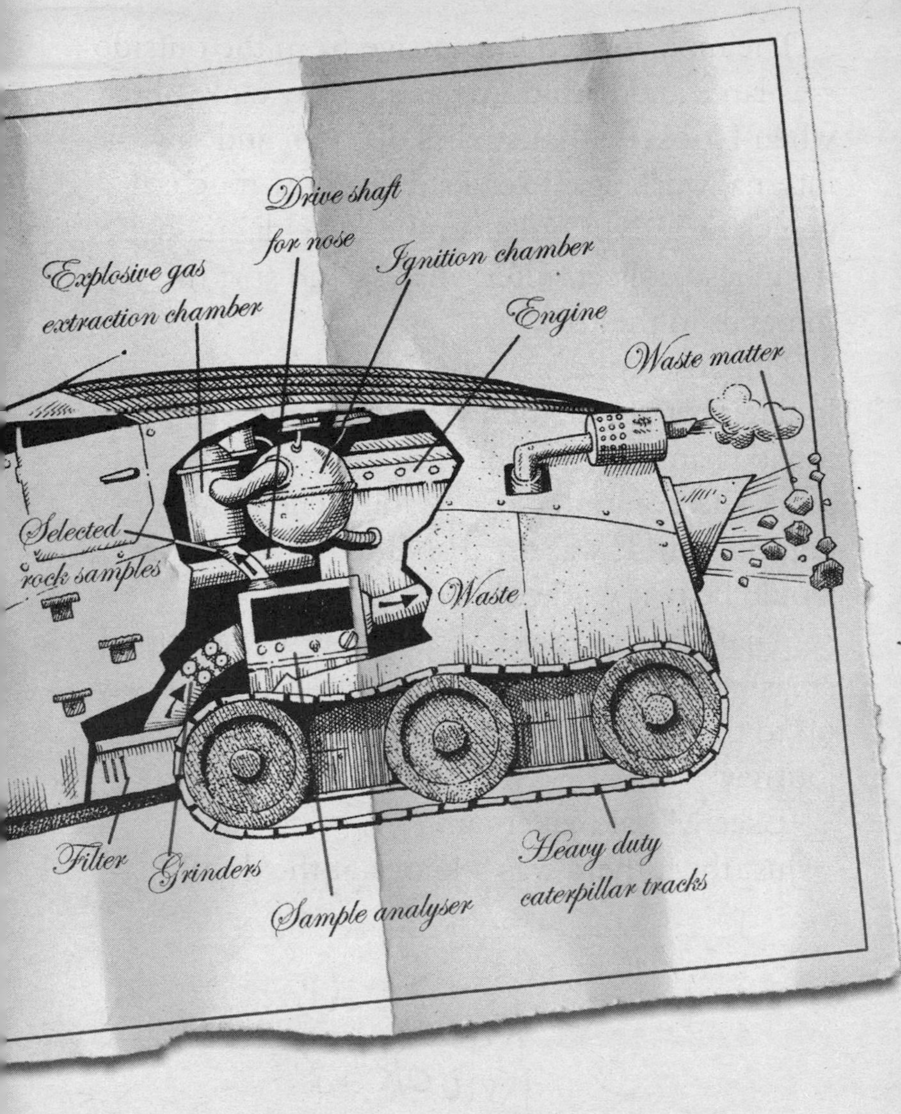

Explosive gas
extraction chamber

Drive shaft
for nose

Ignition chamber

Engine

Waste matter

Selected
rock samples

Waste

Filter

Grinders

Sample analyser

Heavy duty
caterpillar tracks

The mole looked impressive from the outside – as large and forbidding as an army tank – but when I looked at Jakeman's diagram and saw the internal workings, I realized just how much of a genius he is. Not only can the mole dig tunnels, it can also collect, filter, analyse and sort the minerals in the rock.

The nose-cone, armed with its vicious-looking blades, bristled with electronic sensors; it had chambers to take away explosive gases and computers for reading chemical compounds. It was an absolute marvel . . . or would be if it worked!

'That's great,' I said. 'As soon as we've helped smash Craik and his cronies, we can dig our way up to the surface. Then I can get on with my journey!'

'Exactly!' said Jakeman.

Just then, there was a knock at the door!

Tom Returns

Jakeman and I spun round, worried that we'd been overheard by Craik or Bobo; but it was the smiling, muddy face of Tom Baldwin that stared through the barred window!

'You all right, Charlie?' he called. 'Sorry I've been so long – I 'ad to nip off and hide in our secret passage while Craik was in 'ere. When I saw 'im leave with that manky monkey, I followed 'im, 'opin' to pick up some useful information.'

'Did you hear anything important?' asked Jakeman.

'I sure did. I followed them to Craik's own room, and overheard them plottin'. The Shad – sorry, I mean Craik is desperate to have your machine up and working, sir. 'E can sense the slaves are gettin' restless and wants 'is job finished before it all goes wrong.'

'Good,' said Jakeman. 'They're getting nervous. Let's see if we can make things go wrong for them sooner than they expect! Anything else?'

'Oh yes,' said Tom, looking pleased with

himself. 'Craik told Bobo to look out for some scraps, for when they go to feed the Queen first thing in the mornin'!'

'Now that *is* interesting news,' said Jakeman.

'It sure is! First thing tomorrow, I'm gonna follow Craik and find out where the Queen is bein' kept,' said Tom.

'Good idea. If the King knows where she is, he might be able to organize a rescue plan.'

''Ow's 'e goin' to do that?' Tom sighed. 'Everyone in the castle is workin' for Craik, and there's two *massive* Trogs standin' guard outside 'is room.'

'Oh dear,' said Jakeman.

'Don't worry.' Tom grinned. 'I'm goin' to rescue the Queen myself!'

Some News For Me

'Good for you, Tom,' said Jakeman. 'Do you think you can do it?'

'I'll give it a go,' Tom said confidently. 'Oh, and there's one other bit of news,' and he looked at me seriously. 'I heard Craik tell that big baboon Bobo to take you to the mines tomorrow, and to work you extra hard. 'E said it would keep you out of trouble! She looked as if all 'er birthdays 'ad come at once.'

'Oh, flippin' marvellous!' I groaned.

'No, this could be good, Charlie,' said Jakeman, getting excited. 'If the Trogs are ready to fight, and if Tom *can* free the Queen and I can get the mole working, we might have our mutiny tomorrow! You'll be working alongside the Trogs, Charlie; perhaps you could give the battle-cry! I'll bring the mole, and aim it straight at the enemy. They won't know what's hit them!'

'The mole will be working in time, won't it?' I asked, looking at the mess of wires still hanging from the machine.

'Of course,' said Jakeman, looking none too sure. 'But to be on the safe side, best not wait for me. I won't let you down, though. I'll be there, even if I have to push the thing myself!'

'What did you mean about me giving a battle-cry?' I asked.

'You give the signal, Charlie! When the time is right, you give the signal to start the battle!'

'How will I know when the time is right?'

'Keep a lookout for me,' said Tom. 'Eliza 'n' me'll lead the townsfolk to the mine and wait inside one of the tunnels. As soon as we're ready, I'll give you the nod. Keep your eyes on the tunnels.'

'OK,' I said. That didn't seem too difficult. 'But what will my battle-cry be?'

'What about "Smash the Shadow!"?' suggested Tom.

'Brilliant!' said Jakeman. 'Get Eliza to tell the Trogs that the signal will be a small pink boy shouting "Smash the Shadow!" They can't miss that.'

'Too right!' said Tom. 'Look, I've got to go now, it's nearly curfew time. Wish me luck!'

'Take this, Tom,'

I said, pushing my rucksack through the bars in the door. 'It's full of useful stuff and I don't suppose for one minute I'll be allowed to take it down the mines with me. Good luck, mate.'

'And good luck to you,' said Tom, slipping his arms through the straps. 'I'll be back as soon as I've got some news about the Queen.'

The Adventures Of Tom Baldwin

'Scuse my writing. I'm not very good at it. I never went to school for long. And excuse all the mud. My hands are filthy, but what do you expect when you spend all your time down the drains?

Anyway, I found this book in Charlie's bag and he's written up all his adventures in it, so I thought I'd add my own. Phew! This writing lark is tiring. I'm going to have my tea now. Got a nice bit of pastry from the castle kitchens tonight. Lovely!

Oh blow! I keep snapping the end of Charlie's pencil!

My Meeting With Eliza

Well, I got back safe after leaving Charlie
and his mate with their weird-looking machine.
When I got indoors, Eliza was already waiting
as arranged.

'Where's Charlie?' she asked.

''E's been taken by the Shadow,' I said. 'But
don't worry — Charlie's friend 'as got this huge
machine, and 'e's gonna help us. Now, listen
careful . . .' And I told
Ma and Eliza about the
Queen being a prisoner,
and the Shadow being
Charlie's old enemy, and
how Charlie was going to
give the battle-cry.

'I'd better go and tell the Trog slaves then,'
said Eliza.

'Be careful, dear,' said Ma. 'I hate to think
of you out after curfew.'

'I'll be all right,' said Eliza.

'You'll come with me tomorrow, won't you,
Lize?' I asked. 'You know, to rescue the Queen
an' that.'

'Of course I will, silly.' She beamed. 'You don't

think I'm gonna let you 'ave all the fun, do you?
I'll meet you at the mudflats, six o'clock sharp.'
And she slipped out the back door and disappeared
into the shadows of the alley.

Back In the Castle

I got to the mudflats bright and early the next
morning, and Eliza was already waiting.
'Ready?' I said.
'You bet.'
'Let's get goin' then,' I said, and we ducked
into the entrance of the main drain. 'Did you get
to see the Trog slaves last night?' I asked.
'Yeah, and they're really excited,' said Eliza with
a wicked chuckle. 'As soon as they hear Charlie's
battle-cry, they'll go ballistic! And I told 'em
about Jakeman's mole, and not to be afraid of it.'

Soon Eliza and I were inside the castle, creeping
along the corridor to Craik's bedroom. As we got
near, the doorknob started to turn! Bloomin'
heck! I thought we'd had it, but Lize pulled me
into the doorway of the room next door!
'Are you ready, Bobo?' we heard Craik say.

'Good! Let's go and feed the Queen. And be ready for another fiery encounter; she's got more guts than her pathetic King, that's for sure.'

There were cobwebs everywhere

Brilliant – we were just in time!

'Come on, Lize,' I whispered.

'Let's take a look in here first,' said Eliza, pushing open the door to Craik's room and disappearing inside. I followed her quickly. The room was quite bare, except for a bed and a big chest of drawers – and a horrible hangman's noose, standing in the corner!

'Hurry up, Lize,' I said, 'or we'll lose 'em.'

'Won't be a sec,' said Eliza, and darted round the room, opening the drawers and looking under the bed.

'What are you doin'?' I whispered loudly. I was getting fidgety with waiting.

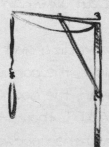

The hangman's noose in the corner. Help!

'Searchin' for somethin' useful,' she said, feeling under the pillows. 'Aha - what's this?' She pulled out a large ring of rusty keys. 'These must be important if 'e keeps 'em under 'ere,' she said, and dropped them in her pocket. 'Come on, let's go, or we'll lose 'em!'

'That's what I-' I started to say, but Eliza was already out of the room.

I dashed after her and we bolted down the corridor after the gruesome twosome, keeping an eye out for guards. Soon we had caught them up, and we crept behind, quiet as mice: down staircases; through deserted halls; across empty courtyards; then out through a door and along a stony track that climbed high above the city and finally led us to a hidden crack in the great cavern wall.

The crack in the rock

the Lock-Up

We followed them inside for about a hundred metres, to where a set of heavy bars divided off the end. In the small space beyond the bars stood the Queen. We crouched behind a rock and watched.

'Let me out, you despicable little man!' she yelled.

'Calm down, madam,' said Craik, smiling. 'There's no need to get your knickers in a twist.'

'How dare you speak to me like that – I'm the Queen. Let me out, I say!'

'As soon as we have finished our work, Your Majesty,' said Craik. 'But there won't be much to go home to, I'm afraid. A quivering husband, a city of half-starved ragamuffins and a land left in permanent darkness. Still, there's no place like home, is

The Queen.

there, Your Majesty? In the meantime, here's
your grub. Bobo, do the honours.'

With that Bobo opened the lid of the pail
she'd been carrying, took out some stale crusts
of bread and flung them through the bars.

'Until feeding time tomorrow, ma'am,'
laughed Craik. 'Ha-ha, ha-ha!'

He turned on his heel and, with his devil
monkey screaming in delight at his side,
marched straight past our hiding place and
out into the great cavern. As soon as they had
gone, the Queen collapsed in a heap and started
to cry, and it was all so bloomin' sad that I
started to cry as well!

'Oh blimey!' whispered Eliza.

the Queen

'Who's that snivelling?' snapped the Queen.
'Come out, wherever you are. Come on, show
yourself.' We stepped out from behind the rock.

'And who might you be?' she asked.

''Scuse us, Your Majesty. I'm Tom and this is
Eliza. We've come to rescue you.'

'Oh, you gorgeous grubby boy and dear

delightful girl, how wonderful!'

I looked at the large padlock that fastened
the door. Flippin' heck, it looked really strong!
'Trouble is, Y' Majesty,' I said, 'I'm not sure
how we're goin' to do it.' I looked at Eliza. 'Any
ideas?'

'How about tryin' one of these?' she said with
a grin, pulling the ring of rusty keys from her
pocket.

She forced the keys into the lock, one after
the other, and tried to turn them.
Nothing happened – but then, with
a loud squeal,
the very last key
started to turn
and the barred
door swung open.

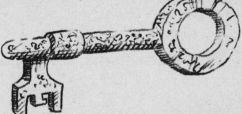

'Said they'd be important,' said Eliza, all
puffed up and proud of herself.

'You splendid children,' said the Queen. 'You're
heroes, both of you, and –'

'Quick, Your Majesty,' I interrupted her,
starting towards the great cavern. 'Follow us!'

Back to the Castle

As we led the Queen down the stony track towards the castle, I told her about our plans for the mutiny against Craik the Shadow and his band of guards. She was well chuffed, and promised to do all she could to help.

'I must talk to my husband about it,' she said. 'Don't worry: if you can get me back to the throne room, I know the perfect place to hide from Craik.'

Twice we had to dodge out of the way when a group of guards passed us, leading a team of Trog slaves off to the mines, but we managed to get safely back to the castle.

Once inside, we padded quietly down the corridors, listening out for sounds of approaching danger. As soon as I could, I yanked out a loose air vent (I'd used this one before!) and Eliza and I led the Queen into the secret passages.

'Well I never,' said the Queen. 'You clever

A Trog Guard.

things! I had no idea about these!'

Soon we were at the grille that looked out onto the throne room, and it was all I could do to stop the Queen yelling out in delight!

Royals Reunited

'Please try and talk quietly, Y' Majesty, or the guards will 'ear,' I whispered.

'Herbert!' called the Queen in a loud whisper. 'Herbert, I'm in here!'

The King jumped out of his throne, looking around the room. 'Hermione, is that you?'

'Don't worry, sir,' I said. 'If you wouldn't mind keepin' yer noise down, I'll 'ave 'er with you in a tick!'

With the dagger from Charlie's rucksack, I started scraping at the plaster around the air vent, listening out all the time for the guards. With the King pulling on the other side, it soon started to come loose, and with a final kick from Eliza, it sprang from the wall with a clatter.

We held our breath, and my heart was pounding fit to bust, but nobody came bursting through the door.

'Thank you, children,' said the Queen as she climbed into the throne room. 'I'll never forget what you've done.'

'Yes, thank you, thank you. Whoever you are!' whispered the King.

'Don't let Craik find you, ma'am,' I said in a low voice.

'Don't worry. There's a secret space below the floor of the throne room. A priest-hole. The Shadow knows nothing about it. He won't find me in a month of Sundays.'

Secret passage

The Queen climbed out of the secret passage and into the throne room.

Throne room.

'And don't forget to tell the King about the mutiny!'

I heard a cry of delight as the King and Queen embraced. I don't know what happened next because Eliza and I were already flying through the secret passages, back to Charlie and his friend Jakeman. As we crossed the great hall, I glanced up the main staircase to check on the guards. Would you believe it – they were fast asleep! So much for keeping quiet!

Tom Returns!

This is Charlie writing again!

I was so pleased when Tom and Eliza appeared outside the laboratory door, but we didn't have long to chat. I was expecting Craik to turn up at any minute and take me off to the mines.

Peering through the bars, they told us how they'd rescued the Queen!

'That's brilliant!' I

said. 'Now the King might join in the mutiny!'

'Sure thing,' said Tom. 'We told 'em all about it.'

'Then let's do it today!' said Jakeman. 'I finished the mole last night, so everything's ready.'

'I'd better nip back 'ome and make sure Ma has rallied the townsfolk,' said Tom. 'Then I'll lead 'em to the mine for the battle.'

'What about the Trog slaves?' said Jakeman.

'I should be able to 'ave a word with 'em when they're changin' shifts,' said Eliza. 'Then I'll nip back and join up with Tom and Ma.'

'Brilliant!' I said. 'You'd better be off. You don't want to be here when Craik and Bobo turn up!' I was beginning to feel really worried. I'd never started a mutiny before and wasn't sure what to expect. Still, I couldn't bottle out now, even if my tummy was churning and bubbling with fear.

'See you!' said Eliza, and they scampered off down the corridor towards the spiral staircase. After they'd gone I realized that Tom still had my explorer's kit. Darn it! Never mind, I'm sure Craik wouldn't let me take it down the mines. I just hope I don't need it!

My pals must have only just made it back to the secret passages in time, because a minute later we heard Craik and Bobo coming.

'Quick, put this in your pocket, Charlie,' said Jakeman, handing me a brown envelope. 'If I can't get to you, or if we're separated, open it. Inside you'll find directions to my factory. I'll meet you there.'

OFF To The Mines

The door burst open and the gruesome twosome entered.

'Right, you,' said Craik, grabbing my shoulder. 'You're coming with us.'

'OK. No need to push,' I said.

'Is that machine ready?' asked Craik.

'Um! Not till to-morrow,' stammered Jakeman. 'It will definitely be finished tomorrow.'

'It'd better be,' growled Craik. Then, putting on his Shadow disguise, he led me out of the laboratory and up the spiral stairs, with Bobo slinking along behind.

I was on my way to the mines!

Working In The 'Light' Mines

We left Craik at the castle, and Bobo drove me before her, over rocks and through passages. After a long and tiring trek, I found myself in a large cavern; just like the one I'd first seen the Troglodyte slaves working in.

Countless numbers of Trogs were dotted about, hammering away at the cavern walls and dragging rubble off in hand carts. Trog guards kept an eye on the miners and flicked their wicked whips if they showed any signs of slacking.

I was put to work with a pickaxe, next to a massive Troglodyte. As soon as he saw me

What a horrible creep Craik is. ↶

he grunted in astonishment. Eliza had told the Trogs to look out for a pink boy, and he knew the revolution was about to happen!

I was given an old stone pickaxe to use.

I looked up at the tunnel entrances. There were about half a dozen – one big one and a few smaller ones – but there was no sign of Tom in any of them yet. I wasn't even sure which one he would appear in. I would have to keep my eyes peeled.

All of a sudden there was a loud, piercing scream in my ear. It was Bobo.

'Get to work, slave,' she yelled in Ape, and nipped at my ankles with her large yellow fangs. 'Get to work or I'll set the guards on you with their whips!'

I lifted the heavy pickaxe over my head and brought it down on one of the rocks.

'*Oof!*' I cried as the axe quivered, sending a judder right through me.

'*Yark!*' squealed Bobo in delight. I heaved it again . . . and again . . . and soon my hands were covered in agonizing blisters.

I hate Bobo. True!

'Work harder, slave!' yelled Bobo.

'Go and stick your head in a hole,' I replied in fluent Gorilla. Bobo screamed with laughter and went racing and hollering around the cavern.

'*Man-cha*,' grunted my huge workmate, staring after Bobo and drawing his forefinger across his throat.

'Yes,' I agreed. 'Bobo is a bad monkey.'

'*Man-cha?*' asked the Trog slave, pointing at me with an enquiring look on his great slab of a face.

'I'm sorry, I don't understand.'

'*Man-cha?*' he asked, pointing again.

Oh dear, this wasn't going to be easy. How can you start a revolution if you can't understand your allies? Then I realized what the huge Trog was asking.

'I'm Charlie,' I said. 'I'm Charlie Small.'

There was a gleam of understanding in his dark eyes. '*Char-cha*,' he grunted.

'Yes, that's right. Charlie.' I grinned.

'Gripmere,' said the Trog, pointing at himself.

GRIPMERE

'Pleased to meet you, Gripmere,' I said, holding out my hand, but just then the thin tongue of a whip thwacked against Gripmere's back and he spun round in anger. A huge Trog guard was standing there.

'*MAN-CHA!*' he bellowed at us, and we quickly got back to work. With a mighty grunt, Gripmere swung his pickaxe over his head and brought it crashing down on a huge boulder, reducing it to powder.

As soon as the guard had moved on, I took a sneaky look up at the tunnel mouths, but there was still no sign of Tom. Then I noticed that Gripmere was grunting to the Trog on his left.

'*Man-cha man-cha, man-cha Char-cha,*' he was saying, nodding his head towards me. Good old Gripmere, he was passing the word along the line, telling his friends that the pink boy was here and to be prepared. At least, that's what I think he was saying! But where was Tom? Where were Jakeman and Eliza? *Hurry up*, I thought. *I can't keep this rock-breaking up for ever.*

Argh! This is one of the vicious Trog guard whips.

Things Start To Happen

I hacked and sweated and carried until my back ached and my arm muscles had turned to jelly, and still there was no sign of my pals.

Then, out of the corner of my eye, I saw a movement in one of the small tunnel entrances and my heart leaped. Surely this must be Tom! But no – my heart sank into my boots again as the monstrous masked figure of Craik came striding into the mine.

My heart leaped!

He marched up to Bobo and started shouting and gesticulating. He paced up and down as Bobo showed her fangs in a horrible sneer and looked over at me with her penetrating eyes. Quickly, I pretended I hadn't noticed them and carried on hammering at my little pile of rocks, but the next minute Craik grabbed me by the shoulders and shook me until my teeth rattled.

'Right, you horrible little pest, where is she?' he snarled.

'Where's who?' I asked, genuinely baffled.

'The Queen, you idiot. Where have you taken her? Tell me now, or you'll find out just how nasty I can be.'

Oh, so that was it! Craik had just discovered the Queen had escaped. Whoops, this was going to be tricky. 'I don't know what you're talking about,' I said. 'I didn't even know there *was* a Queen. And anyway, I've been locked up all the time!'

'Don't give me that, you worm!' yelled Craik, lifting me bodily from the floor. As he did so, I heard Gripmere growl.

'*Yaaark!*' screamed Bobo, baring her teeth in warning.

'I know you must have had something to do with it,' Craik continued, holding my face close to his metal mask and fixing me with his cold eyes. 'Everything was fine before you turned up. I won't let you interfere with my plans again, so tell me – where is she?' He shook me violently again, and threw me to the ground.

Gripmere took a step towards my tormentor. Immediatcly, two guards grabbed him by the arms.

'So, you dare to defy me, do you?' Craik hissed at the uncomprehending Trog slave as he struggled in the guards' grip. 'Take him to the pit. *Man-cha, man-cha*, PIT! Let these fools see I won't be challenged.'

The two guards grinned and started to haul Gripmere away.

'Leave him alone, you pig!' I cried.

By now, many of the slaves had stopped working and were staring over at us, wondering what to do.

'That's it!' screeched Craik. 'I've had enough of your meddling. Bobo – fetch my portable noose. Let's make an example of this interfering boy.'

gulp!

'Oh, yippee!' cried Bobo in delight.

But just as she rushed off, I heard a sharp whistle. It was Tom!

'SMASH THE SHADOW!' I yelled . . . and then it all kicked off!

ALL OUT WAR!

As the Trog slaves turned to face their hated guards, a crowd of Subterraneans surged into the mine from the main tunnel. The townsfolk were followed by a band of mudskippers, and leading them all were the King and Queen!

Tom stood by the tunnel, shouting encouragement. Eliza and Ma and a thousand other Subterraneans followed the King and Queen, and they raced into the big cavern mine.

'Yahoo!' yelled Tom, and joined the throng.

'What's going on?' cried Craik. 'Guards, stop

these pests. *Man-cha, man-cha.* Stop them, I say.'
But the guards were too busy.

The Trog slaves were turning on them,
marching slowly forward, chanting '*Man-cha,
man-cha, man-cha.*'

A Guard and a slave
square up!

The guards tried to push the slaves back with
their whips and clubs, and for one moment I
thought they were going to give in. But no!

With a mighty roar, Gripmere shook himself
free of his captors. Pummelling his chest, he
grabbed a guard in each hand and bashed their
thick heads together. The guards dropped to

the ground, dazed, and the rest of the slaves charged.

Soon there was a mighty battle going on. Everywhere you looked there were Trog slaves wrestling with Trog guards. *Bop! Bash! Crunch! Crash!* The Troglodytes whacked and walloped each other, but their skulls were so thick they hardly felt a thing, and didn't even flinch!

'Let's get 'em!' yelled the King.

'All for one and one for all,' crowed Ma, and Tom, Eliza and the rest of the townsfolk joined in. It was sheer pandemonium!

The King drew a little wooden sword. 'Charge!' he cried, racing into battle. But he tripped over the feet of his tights, which were a little too long for him, hit his head on a Troglodyte's kneecap and knocked himself out!

Charge!

Oh well, at least he had a go; even the Queen was getting stuck in.

'*Aah-aah-aah-aah-aah!*' I yodelled, and dived for Craik's legs, bringing him down in a flying rugby tackle. The horrible mask fell from his face.

'Look!' a Subterranean shouted. 'The Shadow's not a robot. He's nothing special at all!'

'Would you believe it? He's just an outsider!' someone else yelled.

'Look, everybody. Look at the scary Shadow now!'

'Curses!' swore Craik. He fumbled around, putting his mask back on, but he knew the truth was out. The Subterraneans wouldn't be afraid of him any more.

Still spread-eagled on the ground, Craik pushed me away with his heavy boots, and I rolled across the cavern floor.

'Come on, Bobo. The game's up – we've got to get out of here!' he yelled.

But, with a piercing scream, Bobo dived onto my back. She was in a frenzy of rage.

Oof! Get off, you flea-bitten doormat!

Help get this buffoon of a baboon off me!

Is This The End?

Bobo was much smaller than a Troglodyte, but just as powerful and twice as vicious. She clung to my back as I whipped from side to side, trying to throw her off.

I pummelled her with my elbows, but in her frenzy I don't think she felt my blows. Grabbing my shoulder, she flipped me onto my back and I found her staring into my face, her yellow teeth bared in a terrible grin.

'Get him, Bobo!' shouted Craik, getting unsteadily to his feet. 'Finish it now; it's time to go!'

'Not so big without your cutlass, are you, boy?' Bobo screamed at me in Ape. 'Not so high and mighty without Captain Cut-throat to protect you!'

She lunged at me, ready to inflict a mortal wound. Instinctively, I dodged, feeling her incisors graze my neck. One more attack and it would all be over . . . But suddenly a mighty rumble filled the air, and the ground started to shake. Everyone froze in mid-wrestle, staring in the direction of the sound. What on earth was going on? Then, with a huge explosion of rock, a section of the cavern wall disintegrated, and the rotating nose-cone of Jakeman's massive mole, with its diamond-edged spiral blade, rumbled into view.

Jakeman To The Rescue

I could see my friend frantically working the controls, pulling levers and turning valve wheels.

The Trog guards looked petrified, but Eliza had warned the slaves about the big marauding machine, and they cheered at the top of their gravelly voices. All at once, above the noise of the engine, a loudspeaker crackled into life.

'Run!' boomed Jakeman's voice as he turned the cumbersome machine directly at the Trog guards. 'You've had your fun, *now scarper!*'

With a look of horror on their faces, they grabbed boulders and stones, and hurled them at the oncoming machine. The missiles bounced off uselessly, and still the mole thundered towards them. The terrified guards threw down their weapons and raised their hands in surrender. The miners pounded their chests in celebration.

'Watch out!' yelled Tom as a band of scruffers came running into the mine to help their leader. 'They've got reinforcements!'

But the scruffers took one look at the mole, turned on their heel and ran!

A Close One!!

By now, the mole had turned round and was heading straight for Bobo and me!

'Come on, Bobo!' shouted Craik. 'The game's up. Bring the boy and let's get out of here!'

Bobo hissed in anger and started to drag me after Craik by my hair.

'*Yeowch!*' I cried. 'Careful, that's only just grown back!'

Still the mole rumbled towards us, getting closer . . . and closer. *Yikes!* It looked like I could choose between being kidnapped by Craik and being flattened by the mole!

Then, just as the machine was upon us,

Gripmere dived and, grabbing Bobo by the scruff of her neck, lifted her over his head and flung her after Craik. I rolled out from under the squealing caterpillar tracks of the oncoming mechanical monster.

'Careful! That was a bit close!' I yelled at
Jakeman as the mole rumbled past, but he
couldn't hear a word. He just raised his thumbs
and grinned.

Bye-Bye, Craik, And Bye-Bye, Jakeman! ← oh no!

As Craik and Bobo reached the mouth of one
of the tunnels, he turned to speak. He shook his
fist and screamed, but the mole was so noisy we
couldn't hear a word he said.

Just then, with an ear-splitting squeal, the
machine spun round, sending a spray of stones
high into the air. There was a mighty boom, and
a large metal dart shot out of a small aperture
at the front of the mole and whizzed over our
heads.

BOOM!

We watched, spellbound, as the projectile flew across the mine and embedded itself in the rock just above Craik's head.

'Missed!' Craik cried. But he had spoken too soon. A large crack started to snake out from where the dart had landed. It divided and grew, sending out a pattern of smaller cracks across the surface until, with a mighty rumble, the tunnel started to collapse.

'*Aargh!*' yelled Craik and Bobo together, and took to their heels down the tunnel. Rocks rained down around them, and within seconds the tunnel had disappeared behind a wall of debris.

'*Man-cha!*' cheered the Trog miners.

'Hooray!' cheered the townsfolk, the King and the Queen. 'Good riddance to bad rubbish!'

Then, with a metallic squeal, the mole lurched forward again. Jakeman sat staring at the controls, looking confused. His machine was going haywire! In a series of kangaroo hops it headed straight for the wall of the mine. I could see Jakeman pulling levers and turning wheels, but nothing seemed to happen. He looked down from the driver's window and shrugged.

'Wait for me!' I yelled, but the machine

carried on. Its nose-cone started to cut into the rock. 'What are you doing?' I cried. The mole's speaker crackled into life again.

'Charlie, I can't stop it. The engine won't turn off and the brake pedal has jammed. I wired them up when I didn't have my specs – sorry!'

'I thought you'd fixed it,' I called to him. 'So much for your wonderful inventions!' But of course he couldn't hear me.

I leaped onto the mole as it ate into the cavern wall, and grabbed the door handle. Oh no! The door wouldn't open; the mole had already tunnelled too far into the rock.

As it continued to dig, I jumped down from my perch to avoid being crushed. Dumbstruck,

I watched as the machine burrowed into the cavern wall right up to its tail lights. Jakeman shrugged, then waved, and that was the last I saw of him.

'Open the envelope,' came his tinny-sounding voice over the loudspeaker. 'Open the envelope!'

As the mole squeezed into its burrow, a large metal canister was torn from its side. It fell clanging to the ground and, rolling over and over, stopped at my feet.

'*Ouch!*' I yelled, giving it a mighty kick in frustration. 'Jakeman, come back!' But the machine carried on. As it disappeared from sight, the walls started collapsing in on the tunnel behind it. There was no way I could follow it now – there was an almost solid wall of rock between me and the mole.

I couldn't believe it – Jakeman had gone, and I realized I had forgotten to ask him the one BIG question he held the answer to. I still don't know how to get home!

Now what?

The tunnel collapsed behind the mole!

Come back !!!

Jakeman's Envelope

The freed Trogs and the townsfolk danced in delight at their victory.

Tom, Eliza and Ma came over to me; they could see I was upset at losing Jakeman again.

'Never mind, we'll help you find him,' said Tom, handing back my rucksack. 'But what did he mean about an envelope?'

I pulled the envelope from my pocket and tore it open. 'He told me to open it if we got separated,' I said. Inside was a map, entitled *How to find your way to Jakeman's Factory*, and underneath he had scrawled:

I think I might be able to get you home, so make your way to my factory and I will meet you there. Be careful - it's a long and dangerous journey. Good luck and see you soon.
From your pal,
    William Jakeman, Inventor

This is the actual map he gave me:

My factory

←Village

The Wide
Wild River

High Hills

BEWARE!

How to find your way to Jakeman's Factory

I think I might be able to get you home, so make your way to my factory and I will meet you there. Be careful—it's a long and dangerous journey. Good luck and see you soon.

From your pal, William Jakeman
Inventor

As you can see, it's not a very detailed map! Sure, it shows where his factory is, and he has given me a compass direction. Apart from that, it's mainly blank and marked *Unknown and probably very dangerous*. How was I supposed to find my way across that? What's more, it was utterly useless to me if I couldn't find my way out of the Underworld.

Jakeman, you big blithering banana!

What Next?

The whole mine was in an uproar of delight as the celebrations continued! Everyone was hugging and kissing and congratulating each other, and the King led a rousing 'Three Cheers' for Eliza, Ma, Tom and me. The Troglodytes were slapping each other on the back and grunting in joy. Everyone was happy. Everyone except me!

I was still stuck in the Underworld and had no way of getting home. Then, as I stared down at the big metal cylinder at my feet, which had

COMPRESSED AIR

fallen from the back of the mole, I had a flash of inspiration! It might work, I thought. Yes, it might just work! *If only I can find the tubes that first led me into the Underworld.*

'Does anyone know where the tubes are?' I yelled above the din. 'The tubes that lead up above the rocks?'

'Shhh!' ordered the King. 'Let Charlie speak.'

I repeated my question . . . but no one had heard of the tubes. So, that was it, I was done for! Then a lone voice came from a group of freed Trog slaves. It was Gripmere.

'*Man-cha,*' he grunted, turning to Eliza. '*Man-cha, man-cha,*' he chanted, forming simple signs with his big meaty hands.

'Gripmere knows where they are,' she said. 'Craik made some of the Trogs dig 'em.'

'Oh, brilliant! Can he show me?' I cried.

'Of course he can. But *how* are you going to climb up them?'

'If my idea works, I won't have to climb,' I said. 'But there are a couple of things I'll need first.'

Time To Go.

Everyone crowded around me. 'What do you need, Charlie?' they asked. 'What can we do to help?'

'Well, for my plan to work, I need three leather belts, a cushion and a large tablecloth,' I said.

'That's no problem. I'll get them right away,' said Ma. 'It's the least I can do after all you've done for us. Meet you at the castle gates in fifteen minutes.' And off she waddled at top speed.

I picked up the cylinder from the mole and had a closer look at it. Yes, I'd been right. At one end were printed the words COMPRESSED AIR; at the other end was a release valve with a flick switch. That should do the trick, I thought.

'Right, let's get going,' I said, and the whole crowd followed me out of the mine to the castle gates. I was sad to say goodbye to these friendly folk – especially Tom and Eliza and Ma. They had been really good to me. But I couldn't stay underground for the rest of my days. I had to get home.

Before long, Ma was hurrying across the square towards us.

'Thanks, Ma,' I said as I tied the corners of the tablecloth together and folded it neatly under my T-shirt.

'You're welcome,' said Ma. 'Now, wherever you go and whatever you do, take care. Here's some sandwiches. It's not much, and the bread's a bit mushy and damp, but it'll fill your tummy.'

I gave her a great big hug, and she handed me the package.

'Right,' I gulped. 'I'm ready.'

'Can we go with Charlie, to see him off?' asked Tom and Eliza.

'Of course you can,' said Ma and the King together. 'Just be careful.'

Then, with a hearty farewell to the King, the Queen and Ma Baldwin, my two friends and I followed Gripmere across the square and through the narrow streets of Subterranea. With Gripmere now carrying the heavy cylinder, we skirted the shore of the Wide Subterrestrial Sea until we came to a high cliff. Here a concealed entrance led us into a narrow, jaggedy tunnel.

It took ages to get there, turning this way, then that, but eventually I saw in front of me

the tube down which I had first entered the
Underworld.

Rocket Man! Zoom! // ☆☆

Much to the amusement of Tom and Eliza, I
tied the cushion on top of my head with one
of the belts. I then moved my rucksack so that
it hung on my front and tied a length of string
from my explorer's kit to the nozzle on the
cylinder. With the other belts – and Gripmere's
help – I strapped the cylinder, nozzle down, on
my back.

'Right, this is it!' I said, giving Eliza a hug and
slapping Tom on the back. '*Man-cha*,' I said to
Gripmere.

'*Man-cha, Char-cha*,' he replied.

'Good luck, mate,' said Tom as I stepped
under the end of the tube, which protruded
down from the tunnel's roof.

With a final wave and a cheery
'*Cheerio!*' I yanked the piece of
string. The nozzle flicked open, and
an explosive jet of air blasted out of
the cylinder. *Whoosh!* I took off like a rocket!

I shot straight up the tube at a hundred kilometres an hour.

'*Yee-hah!*' I cried. This was better than riding a bucking bronco! Then *CRASH!* I reached the top of the tube, knocking the domed lid up into the air. Thank goodness I'd thought of strapping a cushion to my head, or I'd have been knocked senseless!

The sudden sunlight dazzled me. I flew into the air in a high, wide arc, and up through the clouds. I could see the desert sands pass below as a yellow blur. Then the landscape turned snowy-white as I rocketed over a mountain range. I began to slow, and then drop back towards the ground.

Quickly, I undid the belts around my waist and the cylinder dropped away. As I plummeted earthwards, I unstrapped the cushion on my head and restrapped it around my bottom. Taking the large tablecloth from under my T-shirt, I held the knot and let the rest billow up into a dome above my head like a parachute.

I drifted slowly to the ground, which was now covered with bright green swamp trees, and landed with a bump on my cushioned bottom.

Unexplored Regions!

I have no idea where I am now, but I think I must be slap-bang in the middle of the wild and unexplored blank bit on Jakeman's map!

I appear to be sitting on a small, grassy island. in the middle of a vast and stinking swamp. There are hundreds of islands dotted about the sickly green bog; mangrove trees litter the landscape, and the air is full of strange birds and insects that look as if they might have a very nasty sting!

The map says the factory is in the north-west, but I'm not sure where *I* am in relation to it. I will just have to make a guess, follow my compass . . . and keep my fingers crossed! Of

course, I've got a
bit of island-hopping
ahead of me before I'm
out of this stinking
swamp.

First I want to
phone my mum. It's
ages since I've spoken
to her. I've charged my mobile with the wind-up
charger, and I've got a signal at last!

'Mum!' I said when I heard her voice answer.

'Charlie? Is that you? Is everything all right?'

'Yes, Mum. I'm safe . . . I've been trapped
miles underground in a weird city of mud
people and Troglodytes!'

'Sounds wonderful, dear,' she replied. 'But
don't you think you should get home now?
You've missed your dinner. Just a minute
– who's that knocking at the door? I'll have a
peep round the curtains. Ooh! I don't know
him – some strange chap in a long black coat.
Look, I'd better go and see what he wants. Bye,
Charlie.'

'No, Mum!' I called, suddenly very worried. A
man in a long black coat: surely that couldn't be . . .

Oh no! Surely it can't be Craik
knocking on Mum's door... can it?

'Mum?' I cried again, but she had already hung up. Right, that's it! I've got to get home pronto! But how? I won't know how to get home until I meet up with Jakeman again.

I need to get out of this gloopy swamp and try to make my way to his factory. I hope he made it safely out of the Underworld.

Hold on, what's that noise? The swamp has started glooping and bubbling. Oh no, something's breaking through the thick, slimy surface. *Yikes!* What is it?

A large pointed ear, dripping with gunge; then a sulphurous yellow eye, followed by a wide, warty nose. Now a mouth, open in a loud roar that gurgles like a pot of boiling treacle. A clawed and hairy hand is emerging from the mire and reaching straight towards me. Jeepers creepers! It's some sort of slime monster. Help! Someone, please . . .

PUBLISHER'S NOTE

This is where Charlie's fifth journal ends. If you know where he is, don't forget to tell us at
www.charliesmall.co.uk

Good luck
Charlie,
from Tom

take care
From
Eliza x

Dont do anything silly,
love from Ma Baldwin
x